T0303380

THE PRODIGAL SON

THE PRODIGAL SON

Return of the Assassin

A Novel by

John Burroughs

ELM HILL

A Division of
HarperCollins Christian Publishing

www.elmhillbooks.com

© 2019 John Burroughs

The Prodigal Son

Return of the Assassin

All rights reserved. No portion of this book may be reproduced, stored in a retrieval system, or transmitted in any form or by any means—electronic, mechanical, photocopy, recording, scanning, or other—except for brief quotations in critical reviews or articles, without the prior written permission of the publisher.

Published in Nashville, Tennessee, by Elm Hill, an imprint of Thomas Nelson. Elm Hill and Thomas Nelson are registered trademarks of HarperCollins Christian Publishing, Inc.

Elm Hill titles may be purchased in bulk for educational, business, fund-raising, or sales promotional use. For information, please e-mail SpecialMarkets@ ThomasNelson.com.

Publisher's Note: This novel is a work of fiction. Names, characters, places, and incidents are either products of the author's imagination or used fictitiously. All characters are fictional, and any similarity to people living or dead is purely coincidental. Scripture quotations are taken from the *Holy Bible*, New International Version.

Library of Congress Cataloging-in-Publication Data

Library of Congress Control Number: 2018967535

ISBN 978-1-400324354 (Paperback)
ISBN 978-1-400324422 (Hardbound)
ISBN 978-1-400324439 (eBook)

TO MY WIFE LEE ANNE—

for your belief in me,
for your patience with me,
and for your love for me all these years.

Contents

Prologue   *West Berlin*   ix

PART ONE: LOST   **1**

Chapter 1   3
Chapter 2   17
Chapter 3   22
Chapter 4   34
Chapter 5   40
Chapter 6   51
Chapter 7   58
Chapter 8   66

PART TWO: FOUND   **79**

Chapter 9   81
Chapter 10   86
Chapter 11   93
Chapter 12   99
Chapter 13   107
Chapter 14   120

PART THREE: RECONCILED   **129**

Chapter 15   131
Chapter 16   141
Chapter 17   150

Epilogue   157
Acknowledgements   161

WEST BERLIN

December 1978

From the front seat of his black BMW, Jack Brantley watched as a light snow began falling on the afternoon shoppers walking up and down the crowded sidewalks of the Tauentzienstrasse. He had parked where he could clearly observe the front entrance of the Kaufhaus des Westens and watched as people walked in and out of the massive department store beneath the KaDeWe sign above them. He glanced down at his wristwatch. *One thirty.* It had been a little over an hour since Russell Nash had entered the store and a very tired Jack Brantley was waiting patiently for him to make his departure from it.

He reached over and picked up the thermos of coffee he had brought with him and recalled his long journey back into West Berlin that had begun the night before. He boarded an evening Lufthansa flight in Zurich and landed at Frankfurt just before midnight. A ground shuttle then transported him to the nearby Rhein-Main Air Base, where he sat for three long hours waiting for his credentials to clear. He then hitched a ride on a military transport plane through one of the Berlin Air Safety Center controlled corridors into West Berlin and arrived at the Tempelhof Airport just before dawn red-eyed, weary, and desperately in need of caffeine and something to eat. Two cups of coffee and a bagel got him through a meeting with his section chief and the chief's aide at a small pastry shop at the airport. After they handed Jack the dossier on Russell Nash he took a taxi to his apartment in Steglitz, where a quick shower, some scrambled eggs, and another cup of coffee finally recharged him. He filled a thermos with even more coffee, jumped in the BMW, and drove to the RIAS building on Kufsteiner Strasse where he would wait for Russell Nash to end his broadcast of news from the Free World into the heart of East Germany.

After Russell left the RIAS building Jack easily followed his green Volkswagen Passat through the streets of Schoneberg; it was no surprise to him that Russell drove straight to the KaDeWe. With Christmas Eve and its traditional exchange of gifts just a week away, Jack was certain Russell was planning to enter the store as soon as possible to finish his own preparation for the event and the subsequent arrival of Saint Nicholas the next morning. From the number of people he had observed entering the building, Jack knew each of the store's six floors would certainly be crowded with other like-minded shoppers. He thought of Kelli Newberry and his experience shopping for her last year inside the KaDeWe and was glad he had gotten all that taken care of this year at that quiet little boutique in Paris last month. He glanced at the storefront again and shuddered. *I wouldn't want to be in the middle of that again.*

He reached over to the passenger seat, picked up the dossier, took out a photo of Russell, and reexamined it. *Looks like you put on some weight since I last saw you,* he thought. *You fat pig, I'll bet the first place you headed to was the deli on the top floor.* Reasonably certain that Russell Nash would indulge himself in a huge midday meal before working his way down a couple of floors to shop, Jack settled back in his seat and resigned himself to his fate; it was just going to take a while. It was all good to him. He'd wait as long as it took for the pathetic weasel to emerge.

* * *

The snow had covered the sidewalk completely when Jack glanced at his watch again. *Two thirty.* He detested stakeouts and today's assignment was no exception; the temperature outside was hovering around the freezing mark and he knew the thermometer would only drop further as the afternoon wore on. He was glad he had brought a thermos of hot coffee with him to ward off the cold, and he also occasionally cranked the engine and turned the heater on to warm the interior of the car. He thought about letting the engine idle to keep the heater running continuously but knew that wasn't wise, as it would draw too much attention to himself. *It's going to be a long, cold afternoon,* he thought as he picked up the thermos of coffee, opened it, and poured another cup.

* * *

Two cups later he glanced at his watch again. *Three forty-five.* He drummed his fingers on the steering wheel. *One more cup of coffee and I'm going to have to find a bathroom.*

* * *

Jack's thoughts turned back to Russell. *Why did he sell out to the Russians like he did?* Obviously, money was a motivating factor, but he was certain it went further than that. *There has to be another reason,* he thought. *Something else must have driven him to it. What, besides money, would make a person become a traitor to his country? Was it the woman?* He glanced down at the intel report lying on the seat next to him and picked it up. He flipped to the section on Helga Steiner. *Nothing unusual about her,* he thought as he began reading it again. He looked at her photo once more. *Blond hair, blue eyes. Young. Petite. Very pretty.* He continued reading until something caught his attention; he wondered why he hadn't seen it previously. "Graduated with high honors from the University of Heidelberg. Fluent in English, French, Russian, and German." *Now that's interesting,* he thought. He continued reading. *Nothing at all in here about a current job. Raises a couple of possibilities, doesn't it? Is Helga your latest love interest, Russell, or is she more than what meets the eye? Like, maybe a spy for the Russians and East Germans?* He placed the report back on the seat next to him. He could only hope someone in the agency was keeping a close eye on her.

Jack continued to watch the entrance to the store and thought back to the time he first met Russell Nash. It was at the RIAS Berlin building in Schoneberg a year and a half ago, long before Russell was suspected of selling out to the Soviets. Jack remembered the meeting vividly—Russell came up and introduced himself before anyone had the opportunity to make any formal introductions. *Still don't know how he knew about me, but somehow he did.* He was quite surprised he and Russell hit it off rather well that day; Jack was a loner by nature and hadn't been looking for a friend, but when Russell came along Jack welcomed his company. They would often meet a couple of nights a week for drinks. Jack preferred the quiet solitude of the Rum Trader Bar but Russell gravitated toward the frenetic nightlife and the noise of the Dschungel discotheque. Jack wondered if it was just that he needed a friendly face—an American one at that—and a drinking buddy to vent and let off steam so he often gave in to Russell's choice.

He remembered Russell often telling him how much he disliked the CIA setting him up to pose as one of the American researchers and part-time broadcasters for the RIAS. He told Jack that he was bored with his official duties translating East German and Soviet documents, and that he had put in to become a field operative with the agency but had been turned down more than once. Jack told him he was better off where he was and that his own job as an operative wasn't all that interesting—he spent most of his days doing boring surveillance work and too many nights in too many lonely hotel rooms. "Yeah, Jack," Russell replied, "but at least you're out in the field. That's better than being stuck in that lousy building all day. Besides that, they give you a gun. You get to knock people off."

It has to be more than just the money, Jack thought. *The woman and the money? Add to that not getting the job he wanted—all that must have been what drove him over to the other side.*

The intense cold bore down on him and broke his train of thought. He cranked the engine and let it idle a few minutes before he turned on the heat to warm the interior. He let it run for a few minutes, then switched off the heater and turned off the ignition. *None of my concern, really*, he thought. *Just another assignment.* He replayed in his mind what he was told at the airport coffee shop: *Remove Russell Nash from the equation. Terminate with extreme prejudice.*

* * *

At precisely five o'clock Russell Nash walked out the front entrance and stepped onto the snow-covered sidewalk in front of the KaDeWe. Jack saw that he was holding several large packages in his hands. *Whew, Russell! Just how much of that money you picked up did you spend in there?*

Jack watched as Russell walked down the sidewalk about a hundred meters and unlocked the door to his car. He saw him place the packages on the back seat, close the door, and walk around to the driver's side and get in. A moment later he saw the green Passat pull away from the curb. He started the engine of the BMW and eased out of his space onto the street and watched to see what Russell would do next. The Passat made a quick U-turn and entered the eastbound lane of the Tauentzienstrasse; it was in the direction of Russell's apartment building on the Hauptstrasse and Jack hoped that was his destination. *That's as good a place as any for me, Russell. Hey, I might even bump into David Bowie if he's back from his tour in Japan. I still haven't gotten his autograph since he landed in town last year.*

* * *

Jack followed Russell into the Schoneberg neighborhood to his apartment building on the Hauptstrasse. He parked well north of the entrance to the building while Russell parked closer to the entrance. He watched Russell unload the packages from the Passat and enter the building. Jack glanced at his watch. *Five thirty.* The lingering light of the day was quickly fading into dusk, and the midafternoon dusting of snow had given way to a dense, heavy downfall. He sat in the BMW, enjoying the silence of the snowfall.

* * *

He glanced at his watch again. *Six thirty.* His legs were beginning to cramp from all the sitting, as well as the intense cold. He shifted in his seat and thought about getting out for a few minutes to stretch, but quickly let it pass. *Forget it*, he thought. *It's just too cold out there anyway.* He cranked the engine, let it idle a few minutes, then turned on the heater. *I'll just stay right where I am.* He watched the thick snow continue to fall on the hood of his car.

* * *

It was eight o'clock when Jack spotted Russell Nash walking out the front door of his apartment building. He was smoking a cigarette as he hurried to his car. Jack picked up the handgun from the seat next to him, opened the door, and stepped onto the snow-covered pavement. He walked quickly across the Hauptstrasse, concealing the pistol and the attached silencer behind his back.

Russell had just gotten to his car and unlocked it. As he was opening the driver's door he looked up and saw the shadowy figure of a man approaching him. He took a final drag on the cigarette, dropped it to the ground, and stepped on it. The man slowly emerged from the shadows and the light from an overhead streetlamp illuminated his face. Russell carefully studied the man's features and then said, "Jack! What are you doing here? I thought you were on vacation somewhere in Switzerland, skiing and getting drunk with Kelli."

"I was, until I was called back to town," Jack replied. "Seems there was something pretty urgent for me to attend to. Something that just couldn't wait."

"Well, I'm sorry to hear that, Jack," Russell nervously replied. "When you finally get some time off they go and screw you out of it somehow."

The tension in his voice was palpable. He hesitated and then asked, "So what's so urgent that brings you back to Berlin?"

"You, Russell, and what you've been doing on the other side of the wall," Jack replied. "I went through a lot of trouble to get here to see you."

Russell let go of the Passat's door. "Well then, I hope it was worth it, old buddy."

Jack brought the gun from behind his back and aimed it at Russell's chest. He held it there and said, "It was." He paused before adding, "Tell me something, Russell. Why did you sell out to the Russians? Was it for the money? The woman? The job? *What* made you betray your own country?"

"The money and the job, Jack," Russell replied, looking at the weapon in Jack's hand. "Helga's got nothing to do with it. Everybody thinks she does, but she's just someone I buy things for so she'll sleep with me." He paused, then looked up at Jack. "It's about the money, Jack. And that worthless job they put me in at the RIAS. Friggin' agency, keeping me locked into thirty grand a year! Can't do much with that lousy salary." He paused again. "You know how many languages I speak, besides English? Five, Jack. *Five.* All that time, all that money I spent at Princeton working my butt off. Then along comes the CIA with all those wonderful promises of theirs that didn't amount to anything. After four years over here all I have to show for it is a lousy, stinking thirty thousand a year! And I didn't sell out to the Russians, Jack. I handed everything off each time to some guy from East Berlin named Fritz. He's East German, Jack. *Not* Russian."

"Don't be so stupid, Russell," Jack said. "Whatever you sold to this Fritz guy just went straight to Moscow. You know as well as I do he passed it along to some KGB agent who probably shipped it off to the Kremlin the same day."

"Yeah, well, it's not like it's some secret formula I gave them," Russell said. "Just paper, Jack. Schedules. Memos. Agendas. Nothing vital as far as I can tell and—"

Jack interrupted him. "That's not how I heard it, Russell. I was told you passed along a copy of the president's directive on the SALT II talks next month. Don't know how you got your hands on it, but somehow you did. It ticked off a lot of people at the agency. Including me when I found out about it."

"And so they sent you to find me," Russell said. "Would have thought they'd send someone a little bit older. A little more *seasoned*, maybe."

"Doesn't matter who they send as long as the job gets done," Jack replied. He paused, then said, "You sold your soul to the devil, Russell."

"Maybe so, but I made a lot of deutsche marks doing it," Russell said. "I made sure Fritz paid with *West* German currency, Jack. Not that worthless East German paper." He flashed a smile, then added, "Listen, Jack. I can cut you in on the deal. We can go seventy-thirty from now on. What do you say?"

Jack kept the gun aimed at the center of Russell's chest. "Won't work, Russell."

"Then how about sixty-forty?" Russell asked. He paused, waiting for Jack to respond to the new offer.

Jack said nothing. He only shook his head from side to side.

"Man, it'll add up after a while," Russell said. "A heck of a lot more than what the CIA pays. We deserve more for all we do for the agency. You know good and well what it really costs us."

"We both knew the price of the ticket before we got on the ride," Jack replied.

"Go to hell, Jack," Russell said as he reached into his coat pocket with his right hand and pulled out a Smith & Wesson .38.

Before he could raise it two muffled rounds from Jack's Walther PPK .380 tore into the center of Russell's chest and sent him sprawling backward onto the snow-covered pavement. Jack walked around the Passat's open door and stood quietly over Russell's outstretched body. "Lousy traitor," he said as he took aim at the man's forehead and emptied a third round into the space between his eyes, just above the bridge of the nose. Blood began to pool on the pavement beneath Russell's head; it was soon covered by the thick, heavy snow that fell from the black sky above.

Jack Brantley turned and walked around the front of Russell's car, trampling the fresh snow under his feet with each step he took. *I need to get out of this business*, he thought. *Can't trust anyone anymore.* He removed the silencer from the barrel of the Walther PPK and put it and the pistol in his lower outer coat pocket. *I think it's time to get back to the States again.*

As he returned to the darkness beyond the reach of the streetlamps he thought of Kelli Newberry and how she'd react when he told her. There would be an argument, of course. He knew he'd calm her down, knew they'd quietly talk. He would ask her what her plans were, but he already knew the answer. She'd stay. Of course she would. She was far too wrapped up in her job at the American consulate to ever leave West Berlin.

Let her stay if she wants to, he thought. *Doesn't really matter. I'm done here.*

Jack pulled the collar of his coat tighter around his neck and stuffed his hands in the outer pockets. As he trudged through the deepening snow an image of the fishing pier that jutted out into the Gulf of Mexico from Pensacola Beach flashed in his mind's eye. He smiled. He no longer felt so cold.

He pictured himself on the end of that pier, under a hot Florida sun, with a small group of fishermen looking on in awe as he reeled in one king mackerel after another from the warm Gulf water below.

At his side were his younger brothers, cheering him on, as well, wishing their father was present to admire the catch. Jack admonished each of them; older brothers were allowed to do that. *He's right here with us, guys!* he imagined himself saying to them.

Though he was so far away, on a snow-covered Berlin street, Jack Brantley was already home.

PART ONE

LOST

CHAPTER 1

J ack Brantley stepped out of his apartment onto the shaded second-floor breezeway and immediately noticed how cool and crisp the air felt. The heavy overnight rain had ended early enough that morning to leave the air clean and free of humidity, and as he walked to his car he breathed in the faint aroma of azalea, wisteria, and Japanese magnolia. A brilliant sun was hung midway in the deep-blue, cloudless sky above him, and as he got in his car he immediately reached for his sunglasses for relief from its glare. He started the engine, backed out, and pulled through the gate of the apartment complex and stopped to wait for the traffic to clear. It occurred to him this would be one of those rare, picture-perfect days for driving, so he reached over and pressed down on the power switch to his left. As he pulled out into the thick traffic the cool air rushed in through the open windows of his Camaro, and he inhaled it into his lungs in great gulps and felt vibrant and alive again. He never tired of the springtime in Florida; it was his favorite time of the year.

Though he found the traffic along the road running about the same as it usually did this time of day—thick and congested, slowly inching its way past the hospital, the crowded shopping mall, and the many businesses that stood on both sides of the road—he was determined to remain calm and not lose his temper, as he so often did. *It's just too nice a day to get ticked off*, he thought.

The nearly twenty minutes it took to drive the next two miles completely tested his resolve; he was quite pleased at how calm he had remained through it. When he finally made it past the sprawling campus of the junior college on his right and through the last two back-to-back traffic lights on the crowded highway, he came to a sudden stop at the light that hung above the broad intersection at Langley Avenue. He signaled to turn, made a right, and drove along the northern fringe of the airport, past the clusters of neighborhoods that broke off to the left and right sides of the street. He followed the road as it turned east toward the bay, and crested the hill that rose above the shore of the bay. He let the Camaro drop down the long hill until it came to a stop where the road dumped into Scenic Highway. He signaled to turn and waited patiently for the oncoming traffic to clear.

Almost two minutes went by before he saw a break in the traffic that sped by him in both directions; he gunned the engine and quickly turned left onto the highway. The road hugged the shoreline of the broad bay and Jack's Camaro flowed along with the rest of the northbound traffic on the highway. Within a few minutes he came to a stop at the light in front of the combination convenience store/Dairy Queen that backed up to and overlooked the dark-grey waters of the bay from a cliff-top perch. As he sat waiting for the light to change, he noticed the parking lot was full as usual; people often lingered in the lot after they finished their business inside to enjoy the view of the northern reach of Escambia Bay as it stretched out below them. When the light finally released him, Jack punched the accelerator and the Camaro surged forward. He turned left off the highway and followed the looping entrance onto the eastbound ramp of Interstate 10 and quickly merged with the flow of the thick traffic that crossed the bridge spanning the deep, grey waters of the bay.

It took him just a few minutes to cross the three-mile-long bridge; when it ended it spilled its traffic unceremoniously onto the concrete roadway that ran eastward across the sandy Avalon Beach peninsula. Jack ignored the first exit after the bridge, choosing instead to wait for the second one to appear a few more miles ahead. He hoped the county road running north from that exit would have far less traffic at this time of day; if so it would take him quickly through the quiet hamlet of Bagdad and then onto the busier streets of Milton.

He made his way along the nearly empty streets of Bagdad and turned left onto U.S. 90. He entered the heavy traffic on the wide four-lane highway that ran east and west through Milton. Unable to move into the left lane to pass, Jack was forced to follow a very slow-moving white VW Beetle for the next half mile until he was free to make a right turn onto Highway 87. That road took him past a mix of small businesses, shopping strips, and a sprinkling of wood-frame houses on each side of the road until it began its run along the northern fringes of the small panhandle city. He made it a point to keep a cautious, wary eye on the speedometer while traveling this route, to be certain he was just under the posted speed limits. Though he lived in Pensacola, he was well aware of Milton's reputation as a "speed trap." He made it a point to exercise caution when navigating its roadways. Rumor had it the county sheriff ordered his deputies to sit in their patrol cars on the city's roadways, face the oncoming traffic, and fill their citation books before they ended each eight-hour shift. Jack figured that's the way most small towns and counties operated, and if he was careful enough he could stay out of those books and stick to his schedule. *No use getting mad about this, either*, he thought. *It is what it is.*

* * *

He had been on Highway 87 for several minutes and was well past the road that jutted off to the right that led to the naval base at Whiting Field. He thought it strange not to have seen a sheriff's deputy up to this point. *Maybe they're tied up on U.S. 90, on the west side of town, over toward Pace,* he thought. *It's all under county jurisdiction anyway. Must be more opportunity out there to fill up those books today and get them to cough over their money. Not mine. No, sir.*

To be on the safe side he held his speed just shy of forty-five until he saw a new sign; he gently pressed the accelerator and watched as the needle on the speedometer climbed to a more respectable—and legal—fifty-five miles an hour.

He soon found himself farther along, as the highway stretched out to make its way north alongside the western boundary of the Blackwater River State Forest. It wasn't long before he spotted a patrol car; he knew from its white-and-green markings it was a Santa Rosa County Sheriff's patrol car approaching him from the north. He glanced down at the Camaro's speedometer, and saw he had let it creep up to nearly seventy. *Man! How did I let that happen?* he thought as he eased up on the gas pedal and slowed to the posted limit.

He had heard the sheriff's department updated all its vehicles and figured this would undoubtedly be equipped with a radar gun on its dash. If it was, the cop inside would have it trained on any oncoming vehicles from the south, and Jack cursed at himself for not paying attention to his speed. The probability that the cop would quickly turn around and follow him with his blue lights flashing was great; a stop would completely throw him off his schedule. He had hoped to avoid any confrontations with the law on this trip but was confident if it went that way he was adequately prepared. His license and insurance card were in order, and the vehicle's registration was above his head, clipped to the back of the sun visor. *Everything will be fine,* he assured himself. *Eddie hasn't let me down yet. Let's just see how this thing plays out.*

Eddie Trask did a lot of work for Jack Brantley; he was one of the best forgers Jack had ever known. The confidence level he had in the documents Eddie had prepared for him was unusually high and Jack knew the license, insurance card, and vehicle registration bearing the name of Robert Tilton of New Orleans, Louisiana, were all impeccable. *Eddie, you better not let me down this time, either.* Jack knew Eddie staked his reputation—and his life—on the quality of his work. He remembered Eddie once telling him, "Jack, in this business if I mess up I'm a dead man." He figured that wouldn't happen. He knew Eddie Trask wanted to live a long, long time.

Jack waited to see what would happen next. Best case scenario: the cop would get out of the cruiser, approach Jack's Camaro with professional courtesy, ask him for the necessary documentation, return to the car, and call in the license and registration. Trusting that Eddie Trask did his job well, everything would come back clean and he'd get a ticket citing a violation of some Florida statute with a notation of Seventy in a Fifty-Five Zone. He'd be asked to sign the ticket and forced to wait as the cop would tear it off, hand it to him, and smile as he recited the usual "Have a nice day, sir." With another ticket for the books and his daily quota the cop would walk back to his patrol car, get in, and drive off. That's the way it's supposed to go down.

Then there was the other scenario—the way it *wasn't* supposed to go. If the documents *didn't* check out clean. Jack reached over to the glove compartment and opened it and placed his hand on the Colt .45 automatic, satisfied he was quite ready if it went that way. He checked the gun. *Locked and loaded.* Just like the LT back in 'Nam had taught him. "Lock and Load" Second Lieutenant Richard L. Hackett was always pleased with Jack's readiness for any and every situation. *God rest his soul,* Jack thought. *That man sure trained me well.*

He glanced in his rearview mirror to see what the cop in the patrol car would do next. Suddenly he felt an uneasy sense of déjà vu. Something he had repressed for so long suddenly came to mind. After the tingle up and down his spine went away he thought about it again; he began to recall the details: getting off I-75 at the Tifton exit, just after the hit up in Macon last year, traveling through some small-time south Georgia county, just trying to get to I-10 and then head home to Pensacola. *And that stupid county deputy just had to be sitting there, off to the side of the road, just before I would have crossed into Florida. Pulled me over. Said I was doing seventy in a forty-five zone!*

He shuddered again when he saw it happening in his mind's eye. It had spiraled downward so quickly—a routine stop turned into something he had not anticipated. It wasn't like him to be caught off guard like that, and it angered him even now as he recounted it again. He should have

7

just gotten a speeding ticket and been on his way; instead a cop was dead with two .45 slugs lodged in his chest. The *Tallahassee Democrat* covered the killing, of course, as did the *Florida Times Union* in Jacksonville. The *Pensacola News Journal* even picked up the story. Jack remembered reading the headlines and the accompanying stories in the papers that "a massive search was underway by authorities in several states for the killer of Deputy Trent Holloway."

He hated taking the cop's life like that—it wasn't part of the plan. It was just one of those necessary evils that came with what he did for a living. He hoped he wouldn't have to do it again with this cop, but he knew he would if it came down to it.

Jack glanced in the rearview mirror again, watching as the rear lights came on the patrol car as the cop tapped his brakes while rounding a slight curve a half mile back on the highway. He continued to look in the rearview mirror as those same brake lights went off and the patrol car remained on its steady southward route. *Maybe the radar gun wasn't working today*, he thought. *Lucky for you, bud.*

* * *

Jack continued his drive north on Highway 87. The two-lane blacktop twisted and rose and fell as it made its way through a thick forest of slash pines that stood tall and green-capped against the cloudless blue sky. He noticed the freshly mowed grass lining both shoulders of the road, and his eyes followed a few of the red clay logging roads that broke off intermittently to the right and left of the highway, only to fade into the thick forest. As much as he'd always gripe about the time it took to get to the interstate, he liked this part of the road, as well as a couple of other quiet, less-travelled state roads that ran out of Pensacola and Milton. Though he preferred to stay on the east-west run of I-10, as most of his jobs took him to Tallahassee or Jacksonville or Mobile or New Orleans, sometimes a contract would take him on a run like this up to Montgomery, maybe as far as Birmingham, or over to Macon or even to the Atlanta area, and he'd use this road to take him to Interstate 65 to get him there. For the most part, however, he preferred the jobs that kept him close to the coast. But it wasn't always his choice, and he accepted that. He went where the job took him, where the money was to be made. Price was important, but control over the when and where was also paramount to him.

He declined the numerous international hits that were always offered to a man of his skills and talent—he had had enough of them in his time with the CIA. Those hits took him to so many far-flung places throughout Asia and Africa and Europe that he had long forgotten their names. He left the employment of the CIA, and because he had been careful with his money he had padded several lucrative bank accounts and he had returned to the states with a stake big enough to become an independent contractor. He made a vow to himself he would contract exclusively in the southeastern U.S. and he'd live in and operate out of Pensacola. Who would look for, or even expect to find, a man of his caliber and skills in a small Gulf Coast city like that? And in his own hometown? He figured he was safe, as long as he was careful, and he knew from having grown up there it was a good place to live. Most of all, it was a great way to simply stay under the radar.

***

Boredom from the lonely drive soon set in. To break it, at least momentarily, he made the decision to ignore his cardinal rule about the speed limit. At least until the state line. After all, he *was* way out here in the boonies, Deputy Barney Fife was probably back in Milton now and Deputy Chester What's-His-Name was probably over in Jay getting a donut at a convenience store. *Go for it, Jack*, he thought. *Test her out again.* He pressed the accelerator to the floorboard and the Camaro Z28's hundred eighty-five horses were unleashed from their harnesses. The vehicle immediately came to life under him, charging forward along the road as it took on the climb up a long, steep hill. The thick and profuse pines at the bottom of the hill swept by, quickly giving way to a much thinner stand of pines that was mixed with sourwood and water oaks and dogwood at its crest, and Jack eased off the pedal and brought the vehicle from ninety-five back down to sixty and held it there. He loved the car's power and smooth handling, but knew he had to keep the horses under control always. He kept his life like that, also, and it had fared him quite well up to now.

***

Jack calculated he had a little over an hour before he would hit Interstate 65. Nothing much to do now but think, so he let his mind wander a little while and he began to think of his father and his father's older brother Walter, who had become his favorite uncle. He remembered when he was a boy and they took him into woods such as these and had taught him the names of the trees and the animals that made their homes among them. And then came those fall and winter days, when they had taught him how to hunt and kill some of those same animals. That was when he felt most alive, when he was in those woods hunting, when he began to kill quickly and effortlessly, and he came to the realization that he enjoyed it all too well. He remembered the time he told his father and Uncle Walter how much he liked it, and it had disturbed them greatly. The ensuing conversation quickly digressed into anger on their part, and he knew they just did not understand him. He thought about what they had called it then. "Bloodlust," they said. And then, "Boy, you got to show some respect for these woods and them animals," Uncle Walter once admonished him. His father piped in shortly thereafter. "You kill one more songbird, Jack, and I'll take away that rifle of yours." Jack remembered he quit killing the sparrows and mockingbirds, but not the blue jays. No one liked them anyway.

What he remembered most was how he resented his father's and uncle's efforts to try to change him and shape him into something else. They wanted him to be like them, killing only for the meat that would fill their freezers. *That's okay for them*, he remembered thinking. *But not for me.* He was different and he knew it. He remembered he didn't fret over it too long, because graduation came along and he was free of high school *and* them and, thank God, along came the Vietnam War. Jack didn't wait to be drafted. Instead he signed up in June, found that he tested out accordingly, and after basic training he discovered one of those prized green-colored berets fit his head quite well. He loved it so much he did two tours in Vietnam. He would have done a third but the CIA came calling. Looking for "talented people with special skills," they gave Jack what he was looking for—a way to make a good living and a great deal of opportunities for him to kill for the thrill of it, for the adrenaline high. Uncle Sam didn't seem to mind at all.

The CIA honed his talent and skills to machine-like efficiency over the next six years, and Jack became one of the best assassins in recent memory. But he grew tired of their agenda, their rules, the endless travel, and living out of a suitcase. *No one to trust but yourself,* he thought. *Like Russell Nash.* After two tours in Vietnam with the army and six years with the CIA, he'd had enough. He quit and became an independent contractor, to play by his own set of rules. *The money's still good, and nothing beats being back in the states.*

He thought of these things, and others, as he drove along the lonely stretch of highway. After a mile or so past the crest of the long hill, the state forest ended and the land opened to reveal a few small farms that lay on both sides of the highway. Long, green rows of soybeans and cotton grew in this soil, and here and there someone grew corn and sorghum in the fields that were surrounded by the thick stands of pine that separated one field from the other. As he crossed the state line into Alabama, these fields were broken here and there by patches of land that recently had been cut clear. Piles of jumbled and twisted timber lay in those fields, ready to be chipped or burned and for the land to be turned into more fields of cotton and soybeans. *Somebody actually does this job for a living,* he thought. He wondered what those same people would think if they knew what he did, how he made his living, but it made no difference really. He was paid quite well to do what he did and, apparently, there was plenty of it out there to be done.

***

It was late afternoon when he reached the interstate north of Brewton and he turned onto the entrance ramp and quickly merged with the northbound flow of traffic. The highway rose and fell through this rural area covered by more thick pine forests, and high, billowy white clouds now filled and drifted across a sky that not long ago had been so clear and deep blue. As he clicked off the miles heading north and northeast, Jack noticed those clouds had begun to thicken and turn a dark, lead grey. *Rain up ahead*, he thought. Slowly the land rose higher and the pines gave way to a mix of hardwoods that lined the ridges on the left and right sides of the interstate. Exit ramps broke off occasionally, leading to small towns east and west of the interstate, but their names meant nothing to him as he read them. He was watching for the exit that led to a particular town where he would find a particular resident of that town and deal with him according to the wishes of a very particular client of his.

The exit leading to the one he wanted came faster than he had anticipated, and he entered the off-ramp for Fort Deposit. Jack quickly decelerated and pulled up to the stop sign. He was told the intended target could be found at this time of day at his home just west of the exit, and so he turned left onto the two-lane county road and looked for the small, white, wood-frame house and the owner's white F-150 with its Rebel Flag license plate mounted on the front bumper. As he drove along the road searching for the man's residence Jack opened the glove compartment, pulled out the .45 ACP, and laid the pistol next to him on the passenger seat.

Dusk was closing in, and the lead-grey clouds overhead began to release their load, and the rain began to fall, softly at first, then heavier and thicker, pelting the hood and roof of his car. He was confident he'd find his intended target soon and would deal with him accordingly. Rain or shine, it didn't matter, especially after what he went through back in those rice paddies and villages and jungles in 'Nam. He recalled what the lieutenant told his men before each mission: "Just get the job done. Watch each other's backs." And with deadpan seriousness he would add, "And don't make me have to drag any of your butts outta there." Jack and the others on his team had no problem taking out the VC, and even the local villagers they came across who all too often lent their support to them. The LT was a hard man, loved and respected by his men because he genuinely loved and respected each of them, as well. Jack reasoned if the LT were alive today then he would probably have a real problem with this hit, especially since the intended target of the day had also seen action in Vietnam. This posed a slight issue with Jack when he had read the details, but he quickly let it go. He remembered thinking, *Not everyone who wore Army green gets off easy back in the states.* He had to admit he did wonder what this guy must have done for somebody like him to come way out here in the middle of nowhere, and he had wondered what his reaction would have been if the hit was to be done on a former Green Beret, but those thoughts quickly passed. *None of my concern anyway*, he concluded. *My interest in this matter is strictly business. Just like all the others.* He repeated the LT's mantra out loud. "Just get the job done." There. It's said and done.

***

When it was finished—and he was on the long drive southward on the interstate, and he was wet from the heavy rain and had used a towel to dry himself off and he had thrown the towel on the floorboard afterward and he had turned the heat on low, just enough to keep from shivering— Jack began to think about what had happened. How it went down back there wasn't according to plan. He found it puzzling to be so troubled after this hit. He found it hard to shake the memory of it, seeing it so clearly in his mind. It was as if he were detached from himself, observing it as if he were a spectator on the sidelines, watching what was unfolding.

He replayed the scene in his mind. This hit was going to bother him for sometime...

The three-hundred-and-fifty-pound man lumbered toward Jack as he fired into him. Two quick shots, the first in the man's chest, near the heart, and the second right at the heart, but the huge man somehow just kept coming. Like some wild animal intent on killing what was killing it. Jack had placed his shots carefully, yet the man did not go down. Jack's next shots were to each of the huge man's kneecaps, and the man finally fell to the ground, only to continue moving forward, crawling over the rain-soaked ground. Jack watched in amazement, and in awe, as the man willed himself forward in the mud toward Jack. Finally, exhausted and with his life ebbing from him, the huge man stopped and quit breathing and was still. Jack walked up to the prone body, knelt, and with a great deal of effort rolled the heavyset man on his back. Jack stood and fired a final round into Fat Man's forehead, just above the bridge of the nose. He retrieved the empty casings, walked back to the Camaro, started the engine, turned the vehicle around on the muddied ground, and pulled back onto the road and drove eastward, back toward the interstate.

. . .His forehead and hair still felt wet. Jack reached for the towel again and dried himself once more. *My God, man! How did you get so fat?* he thought as he continued his drive southward, toward home. *One, no more than two shots and all the others would go down. But not you! Two more in the kneecaps and yet you still kept coming. Crawling, but still moving.* Jack wondered what Fat Man would have done had he reached him, and was glad he hadn't. The picture he had been given of the man must have been five years and a hundred pounds ago. Jack made a mental note to be a little more demanding in the future. He'd make sure he would get more recent photos of his assigned and intended targets. *Err on the side of caution, and avoid surprises at any cost*, he remembered the LT telling him. Jack figured the LT would forgive him for this oversight as long as he learned from this mistake.

Jack pulled off the interstate, onto the exit leading to Flomaton, and then drove back across the state line into Florida and onto the four-lane highway that led south to Pensacola. A wave of relief came over him, as if crossing the state line somehow allowed him to be able to handle and deal with it. The thoughts and images of Fat Man, for the rest of the drive back to his apartment, could somehow be put aside, at least for now. It would be expected of him to handle it, both by himself and by his client. Not that he'd let his client know the hit troubled him like it did. After all, he was "Mr. Cool." That's the label they stuck on him, in Vietnam and then in the CIA. There were a few other names and titles bestowed on him, mostly from other platoons. He only heard about them; they were never spoken to him face-to-face.

Then there was the one that army shrink had laid on him. Jack remembered it vividly. While he was a Green Beret, on his last tour. It had come on the heels of one of those many "incidents" that happen in war, in one of those obscure villages where they seem to always take place. But this one was different, and was legit as far as Jack was concerned. *If only that lousy shrink knew the full story about that VC double agent,* Jack thought. *He might not have agreed to what took place, but he would have at least understood.* But he didn't, and then came the shrink's official report after the numerous sessions Jack was forced to undergo. *How did that report go?* Jack thought. *Oh yeah: "It is my professional opinion that Specialist 4 John Thomas Brantley, of the 5th Special Forces Group, Company D, harbors deep-seated sociopathic tendencies and behavioral patterns. . . His actions could be construed as borderline psychopathic in scope and nature. Furthermore. . ."* Blah, blah, blah. That shrink didn't know anything. Sitting in his air-conditioned office in Saigon, *analyzing me!* Overeducated egghead! But none of it mattered anyway. What mattered most was that Specialist 4 Jack Brantley got the job done. And that he, "Mr. Cool," "Jack the Man," could be counted on when it all broke loose. Besides, the LT had ordered the execution, and Jack *always* followed orders.

No one in the company revealed the LT's role in the death of the VC agent, nor would they. Jack endured the negative aspects of the report out of respect and admiration—and love—for the LT and his reputation.

Even when the lieutenant was killed, the secret remained. All the men in the company agreed to it. Swore they'd never reveal they were ordered to do it. Jack was the trigger man, and didn't mind doing it. Didn't mind it in the least. *That filthy, double-crossing VC got what he deserved*, Jack reasoned. A bullet to the head, and his body dumped in the nearby river. "Sociopath." "Psychopath." *Screw that shrink*, Jack thought. *He didn't have a clue what it was like in-country.*

***

Jack continued driving on Highway 29, south through the small town of Century, and then on through the McDavid community. Up ahead was Cantonment, and then back to his apartment on Ninth Avenue. He did not want to go there, but knew he had to. He would see Fat Man again this evening or some time in the dead of night. He had to face his fears—all of them—once again. He kept those fears to himself, and in doing so he paid a price. No one knew, nor would they ever know, how it was for him when the night came and it was still and he laid in the quiet of his bedroom, waiting for the demons to arrive. They always came. They were relentless, patiently waiting for him to fall asleep, to slip into their world. And it was there those demons would remain with him through the long, dark, lonely hours until dawn.

CHAPTER 2

Jack woke to the distant sound of a dog barking somewhere in the neighborhood behind his apartment complex. Fat Man and the demons didn't come calling last night; he was puzzled by it, but when he shook the cobwebs from his head he was grateful for the uninterrupted sleep. Then he thought, *They must have taken the night off, planning to visit me tonight instead.*

He looked over to the window he had left open overnight and watched as a soft breeze licked the thin curtains that hung on each side of it. He reached over to the nightstand, pulled a cigarette out of the pack, grabbed the lighter next to it, and lit it, then listened to the morning sounds, similar ones that now took him back in time to his parents' house on the west side of the city, to that small, wood-frame house his father so proudly built in the early fifties and where he and his three brothers grew up. He remembered the warm, mid-spring Saturdays when he was allowed to sleep in, when he would wake to the sounds of his neighbors and their dogs, but mostly to the aroma of frying bacon that came from the kitchen. He loved those big breakfasts his mother made for them on Saturdays—scrambled eggs, bacon, and pancakes, with milk for her boys and a big pot of coffee for her husband—and how she would smile that contented smile of hers at the scene of domesticity before her.

He loved those mornings, and longed for the peace they brought him. He thought of the late winter and early spring, when the blood-red camellia blooms burst forth and filled the yard; he also remembered the radiant pinks and purples and softer reds of the azaleas that burst forth not long afterward. His mother had planted those bushes just after the house was completed and then christened by Father De Marco. Watching them grow and burst forth in their vibrant colors caused envy in Edith Brantley's neighbors; they had tried in vain to duplicate her yard and those massive bushes. But their efforts were in vain. She tried to tell them if they would just join "the One True Church" they could get the good Father to bless their house and yard, as well. "I'm sure Our Heavenly Father will see fit to adding to the beauty of your yards then," she would tell them. Jack remembered some of their replies. Things like, "Thank you all the same, Mrs. Brantley, but we'll pass." As much as it hurt her to hear them say that, she let it go, thankful that at least her husband Frank had finally left those "heathen Baptists" and converted to Catholicism.

Jack remembered how his father promised to someday take his mother to Italy, to see the Vatican and the Pope. "Someday, Edith. When the boys are all grown, we'll go," he often said to her. "If it's God's will, Frank, then we *will* go," she would always reply. Jack remembered his father never had the money even after Richard, the youngest, graduated from high school and had joined the Marines. Then there was the accident at work that took his father's life and ended the dream he had of that trip to Italy. He often wondered if Mom still wanted to go after that, even without his father, but then she, too, died soon afterward. "She died of a broken heart," he heard everyone who knew Edith Brantley say. *God, I sure miss those two*, he thought. He made a mental note to go by the cemetery tomorrow afternoon before heading to the gym for a workout.

Jack began thinking of the day ahead of him as he laid there and finished his cigarette. But his thoughts were soon broken by the loud slamming of a car door in the parking lot in front of his building. The car-door-slamming was soon followed by the equally loud voices of the all-too-familiar couple next door to him. He couldn't remember their names, but it wouldn't have mattered if he did. Mr. and Mrs. Loud Mouth began to yell at one another and their bickering soon escalated into another one of their infamous fights as they walked from the parking lot into the breezeway and up the stairway to the second floor and into their apartment. Jack heard their door slam. The walls between his apartment and theirs weren't thick enough to fully contain their heated arguments. He'd already reported it to the apartment management, to no avail, and he had to listen to it again.

"You no good, worthless bum!" Jack heard the woman yell. Jack then heard the man reply "Don't you ever talk to me that way, woman!" That was followed by the sound of another door slamming shut (bedroom, probably), and then Jack heard the muffled sounds of the woman sobbing and the man knocking on the door, and then he heard the man's muffled voice pleading with the woman. "Come on, baby. Open the door." And then it was quiet for a while. Too quiet. Then the moaning soon followed. He laid there and couldn't help but chuckle at the thought of this thirty-something couple making love after another one of their infamous fights.

After a few minutes the moaning ceased. He'd heard too many of their stupid arguments and too many of their doors slamming and too many other things, and he was just plain sick and tired of Mr. and Mrs. Whatever-Their-Names-Were. He chuckled, and thought for a moment, and then he laughed as he pictured the image of them in that bed. *I'd be doing everybody else in this building a favor if I just go over there, bust the door down, and shoot each of them in the head while they're lying there,* he thought. He wondered how much it was worth to the others in the building. *I'll make it cheap. My rock-bottom price for the hits. Maybe a two-for-one special.* He reached over for another cigarette and lit it. *What the heck. I'll do it pro bono, just to have some peace and quiet.*

Jack continued to lie in the bed and finish the cigarette, and then got up to go to the bathroom. He looked at himself in the bathroom mirror, and noted the circles under his eyes had somehow grown darker over the last couple of days. In desperate need of some coffee, he wandered into the kitchen and opened the cabinet above the dishwasher and found the can of coffee. He popped the plastic lid, dumped in too much coffee into the filter of the coffee maker, added the water, and turned the switch to on and stood there in a daze. The gurgle brought him out of his stupor, but it would be a few minutes before he'd be able to pour the first cup that would kick-start his mind and body for the day. He opened the refrigerator and found a half-empty carton of milk. He opened it and smelled it. It was beginning to sour but it would be good enough for the coffee. He looked through the refrigerator again and saw there was some leftover pizza in a carry-out box from a few days ago. He then looked in the cabinet above the sink for other options. He shook the two boxes of cereal he found there. Not much in the Cheerios box. Even a little less in the Golden Flakes. He thought about combining the contents of the two boxes. *Just may be enough to fill a cereal bowl. But how will it taste?* Unsure how that combination would end up tasting, he returned to the refrigerator and pulled out the pizza. *Nothing wrong with a little cold pizza in the morning*, he thought. He extracted a slice from the box and bit into it and chewed as he watched the coffee finish dripping into the pot.

Jack fumbled in a drawer, pulled out a piece of paper and a pen, and started a list of things he'd get at Winn-Dixie over on Davis Highway and set the list by the keys he had laid on the counter last night. First and foremost, he needed the coffee. To wash down the slices of pizza that served as a makeshift breakfast. *Get real, Jack*, he thought. *You want that coffee to kick-start your butt.* Confident that they'd be enough to get him going until he'd go through the drive-thru at Whataburger later in the day, before hitting Winn-Dixie, Jack finished the last slice of pizza and a second cup of coffee. Feeling awake now, he made a mental list of the other things that needed to be done, slightly irritated with himself for letting all of them pile up over the last two weeks. He'd been busy, far too busy to do the things most people somehow found or made the time to do. He'd simply get them out of the way today and tomorrow, and then he'd be busy again with the next job, this time to the west, in New Orleans. He was looking forward to the Cajun and Creole foods that always satisfied his palate; Jackson Square and the riverfront, and especially the ladies he'd find at the bars in the French Quarter who would satisfy his other senses and needs beckoned him, as well. He remembered an advertisement in the Travel section of the *News-Journal*: Come to the Big Easy and Stay a While. He planned to do that very thing, starting Monday morning.

CHAPTER 3

Monday came all too soon, and as planned, he was westbound on Interstate 10. He glanced at the clock on the dash of the Camaro: 11:30. It was much later than he had planned to leave. He had not slept well last night; the demons paid him another one of their visits, and as usual had left at sunrise. He wrestled with them most of the night, through the deep darkness of the early morning, dozing now and again, waiting for them to depart. He had gone back to sleep after they had left, and now he regretted oversleeping. *But hey, it' still Monday morning*, he reasoned. He was just now crossing the bridge over the Perdido River that formed the western boundary between Florida and Alabama, and he knew he could be in New Orleans by midafternoon if he didn't stop. If he did stop for lunch and a couple of breaks, then certainly no later than dusk.

It dawned on him that he really didn't have to rush to get there. He had not planned to make the hit until tomorrow. Today was for the drive to New Orleans. And for other personal matters: secure the rental car, check into the hotel downtown, get a nice dinner, have a few drinks. And try like hell to get a good night's sleep. Enough anyway to take care of business tomorrow and have the rest of the evening for some fun in the Quarter. *Might even stay a couple more days*, he thought. So he eased back in his seat and relaxed, determined to enjoy the ride and have some time to listen to some music and think and plan.

He glanced down at the speedometer. It read just under sixty. *Watch your speed,* he thought. *Keep it right there.* He knew he'd have to be cautious on this stretch of the interstate, more so than his latest venture into the state, as the Alabama Highway Patrol strictly enforced the mandated fifty-five miles per hour speed limit. Their enforcement bordered on an almost religious fervor. He had no encounters with them yet, nor did he plan to. It was much easier dealing with the small-time county deputies who worked far lonelier roads than this. A pull over by a state trooper on this busy stretch of interstate might prove to be a major hassle for him, and he wasn't willing to risk that. Though the Camaro's V8 and all those horses were tempting him to floor it, he held the speed just above the legal fifty-five and figured he'd be better off doing so. So he popped in his ZZ Top *Tres Hombres* cassette, rewound it back to "La Grange," cranked up the volume, and figured it was best to act like just another law-abiding, average citizen driving to Mobile. *Ease on down the road, big guy,* he thought. *You'll get there when you get there. Ain't like you have some nine-to-fiver you just gotta get to.* The soundtrack with "La Grange" started to play. *And watch the horses,* Jack added in thought. *Keep them reigned in today.*

He comforted himself in the knowledge there'd be other times, other days, between contracts, when he could find some lonely stretch of highway out in the countryside north of Pensacola where he could open it up and let them loose again. For now he was content to fall in tune with the beat and the lyrics blasting from the cassette player. *"Rumor spreadin' 'round. In that Texas town. About that shack outside La Grange. And you know what I'm talkin' about. Just let me know, if you wanna go, to that home on the range. . ."*

***

Pastures, farms, creeks, and thick forests of pine flew by him, and occasionally an exit to some small town broke off the interstate. The land rose higher now as hills began to appear as he neared the Spanish Fort exit. He knew from past travels there were some fast-food places at this exit and he momentarily thought about pulling off the interstate and going through one of the drive-thrus there for some late breakfast and coffee, but he decided to keep going and wait until he had gone farther. Make it a lunch stop instead. His bladder was holding out for now, and he figured he'd wait to find one of the other fast-food places west of Mobile. A Hardee's or Burger King or a McDonald's would do just fine for a quick lunch to hold him over until he could delight his senses at one of the many wonderful full-service restaurants to choose from in New Orleans.

He came to the crest of the hill and saw Mobile Bay up ahead, with the interstate spanning its smooth grey waters. A cloudless blue sky sat above the bay and the city skyline to the west, and the Camaro rolled down the hill toward the bay and the long span of highway that crossed it.

Traffic began to thicken as he drove across the causeway; he flowed with it and was glad when he saw the sign TRACTOR TRAILERS EXIT HERE, where the big rigs were forced onto the two-lane causeway to use the old Bankhead Tunnel under the river. He and the other smaller vehicles were allowed to remain on the interstate, and then Jack saw the twin tunnels up ahead that moved traffic east and west under the Mobile River. The Camaro quickly entered the westbound tunnel. The highway dropped slightly and then rose again, and it entered back into the bright sunlight as the road twisted and curved through the downtown area toward the western suburbs and towns of Tillman's Corner, Theodore, and Irvington.

The traffic began to thin out gradually as more and more of the vehicles alongside and ahead of him took various exits into downtown Mobile. Jack continued in the right-hand westbound lane and noticed there were a number of post-Frederic blue roof tarps still on the houses that stood. He also took notice of the many empty slabs where there once had been houses. It was when he hit the Grand Bay interchange and then the Mississippi state line that he noted the real devastation that hurricane did a year and a half ago. He remembered watching the news broadcasts out of Mobile showing how Frederic had slammed into Dauphin Island in the early evening darkness that September and pushed its way inland. He observed many of the tall and slender pines, with their green tops shorn off, standing like matchsticks; many of them remained leaning northward from the fury of the wind that came so quickly from the south. It would be months, perhaps years, before the area fully recovered from the effects of this storm, but the people along the Gulf Coast were resilient and moved on with their lives. *Good for them*, he thought. He applauded their "what's done is done" attitude and admired their tenacity and willingness to rebuild.

***

Jack approached the Moss Point-Pascagoula exit and decided to find a fast-food place now. A sign beckoned him with its message: BURGER KING JUST AHEAD. He pulled off the interstate, decelerated, and slowed to a stop. He turned left onto Highway 63 and crossed under the interstate and saw the HOME OF THE WHOPPER sign a quarter of a mile on his left. Bladder full and stomach empty, Jack quickly pulled into the parking lot, found an empty space just across from the entrance to the building, and shut off the engine. He checked the glove compartment. He knew it was locked, but he checked it anyway. *Better to err on the side of caution*, he thought. He opened the door, hit the AUTOMATIC LOCK button on the door's trim panel, closed the door, and checked the door handle to reassure himself it, too, was locked and secure. He crossed the lot, entered the building, and quickly located the sign for the men's room. He walked down the narrow corridor and pushed open the door, only to find both urinals occupied. At one of them he saw a little boy aiming carefully into it with a tall, heavyset man hovering over him. He noted the toilet stall's door was closed and locked. *Gotta pee like a racehorse and I have to wait*, he thought.

"Come on, Joshua, hurry up and finish," the big man urged the little boy.

"Okay, Daddy," the boy replied. "I'm hurry-in."

JOHN BURROUGHS

The big man turned toward Jack and commented, "Sorry, pal. It takes him a little while to get it done. Hope you ain't in too big a hurry."

"I am, but there's no sense in getting upset over it," Jack replied. "He'll be finished soon enough."

"Okay, Daddy, all done," Joshua said. "You gotta go, too, Daddy?" the little boy asked as he was fumbling with his pant zipper.

"Nah, son, I'm good. But this man here sure looks like he needs to," the man replied. "It's all yours, mister."

"Yeah, it's all yours, mister," Joshua repeated as he continued trying to pull up the zipper on his pants.

Jack smiled at the little boy and watched as the big man tenderly reached down to help his son finish zipping up. When the boy stepped aside Jack took his place, and as he stood in front of the urinal he heard the two of them open the door. As they started out the door he heard the little boy say, "Daddy, Daddy. Can I have a choc-lit shake after I eat my hamburger?"

Jack finished up in the bathroom and went down the little hallway that led to the lobby of the restaurant. He waited in line as a young couple ahead of him placed and paid for their order. He scanned the small crowd of diners while he waited. He quickly spotted Joshua and his dad, and smiled again as he watched the little boy with the paper crown on his head. He saw the boy take the last bite of the hamburger, watched as he chewed it while eyeing the small cup in front of him as he did so. *Probably the chocolate shake*, Jack thought. Joshua finished chewing, swallowed, and turned to his father. Even over the din of the lunchtime crowd Jack could hear the boy clearly.

"OK, Daddy. I'm through with my hamburger now. Can I have my choc-lit shake?"

"All right, son. Go ahead," his father replied.

Jack smiled as he watched Joshua reach for the paper cup and pull it toward him. The little boy placed his lips around the straw and took a long drink of the shake, and Jack watched as the little boy again turned to his father.

"Want some of my choc-lit shake, Daddy?" the boy asked. "It's real good."

"That's okay, son," his father replied. "You finish it. It's all yours. You been a good boy for your mama this week, and—"

Jack heard a female voice from behind him say, "May I take your order, sir?" He turned to see a blonde teenage girl at the counter. She looked past Jack, at the long line behind him, and sighed.

"Excuse me," Jack said. "Sorry, I wasn't paying attention."

"Are you ready to place your order, sir?" she impatiently asked.

"Uh, yeah," Jack said. "I need mine made to order, a certain way. Your guy back there can do that, right?"

The girl at the counter looked at Jack again. She sighed again. Then she seemed to see Jack for the first time, noticing the handsome, clean-cut, well-built man standing in front of her. Her prior impatience and attitude changed dramatically. "You can have it any way you want it here, sir," she added in a slow Mississippi drawl.

Jack knew a flirt when he saw one. He figured he could really have it his way if he wanted it to go that far. But he was here for the food. After all, that's what they were known for: "Have It Your Way." But she apparently had something else in mind. *She's laying it on kinda thick*, he thought. Jack noticed her pale-blue, piercing eyes, eyes that were framed by long lashes. He noticed the perfect white teeth. Eyes and hair and teeth that screamed, "I'm looking for a husband to get me outta here! And you might just do it for me." He had seen so many of them like her, and he imagined her to be one of those girls who had few options available to them, girls who went out and got a job at a place like this, to earn some money but really to flirt and giggle with customers like him as they tried to nab a husband as soon the high school graduation ceremony was over, only to have her first baby at nineteen and be divorced at twenty-one or twenty-two and find herself back behind the same counter, or one just like it at McDonald's or Hardee's. She would end up working wherever she could for whoever would give her the most hours on her schedule so she could feed her babies and go to the local junior college for a second life after having failed the first so miserably. It saddened him to think of her and her future, but it was really none of his business. So he ignored her feeble attempts at flirting, glanced up at the menu to avoid looking into those eyes, and called out his order to her.

"Make it a Whopper. No mayo. Just lettuce, tomatoes, pickles, some mustard. Medium fries, medium Coke," Jack stated. He kept his eyes on the menu board above Pretty Blue Eyes' head. He knew if he looked into those eyes she'd have him. Hook, line, and sinker. Would it matter to her if she knew he was thirty years old to her seventeen, maybe eighteen? *Jeez*, he thought. *She's still in high school.* It may not matter to her, but it certainly mattered to him. Jack wasn't about to get too personal with this one—it was way too dangerous.

"Oh, and add a small chocolate shake," he added. "In honor of Joshua being such a good boy for his mama this week."

Miss Pretty Blue Eyes heard the order for the shake, but the honorarium for little Joshua went straight over her blonde head. That didn't matter. She wasn't expected to catch it, much less know what it was about. He left it at that.

"Will that order be for here or to go?" she asked.

Her tone was more serious now. Having lost interest, the flirting ceased and she turned very businesslike in any further interaction with Jack. She told him the cost of his order. He reached into his left front pocket, extracted a ten-dollar bill, and gave it to her. Miss Blue Eyes handed him his change, and Jack stepped aside to let the teenage boy behind him move forward to place his order. He watched Miss Pretty Blue Eyes' countenance change dramatically as she spoke to the customer who now stood in front of her. Unlike Jack, the teenager wasn't looking up at the menu board. He was staring straight into those piercing blue eyes.

"Hey there, Jimmy," she said. Honey dripped off her tongue as she spoke. "I saw you playin' in the game Friday afternoon. You were awesome. Hittin' those two homeruns. Beatin' Biloxi like ya'll did. That was somethin' to see."

Jimmy blushed, and continued to gaze into her eyes. Prospective husband Jimmy. *Whew!* Jack thought, observing this very un-businesslike transaction taking place at the counter. *Be careful, young stud. She's out to get you. Hook, line, and sinker.*

***

Clutching two carry-out bags in his left hand—one with his burger and fries, the other with his coke and shake—Jack politely held the door for an elderly couple as they were leaving at the same time.

"Thank you, young man," the lady said.

"That's mighty nice of you, son," the man added. "Mighty nice, indeed," he repeated.

They reminded Jack a little of his own mother and father, the way they walked so closely together. The old man held his wife's hand.

"My pleasure," Jack said as he let them pass. He let go of the door and reached into his pocket to extract his set of keys. He watched the elderly couple a moment longer as they walked down the sidewalk in front of the restaurant, hand in hand, heading toward their car. He then turned away from watching them and started toward his own car. He saw two baseball-capped, T-shirted young white men, probably early to mid-twenties, standing beside the Camaro. T-shirt number one, his head covered by a New Orleans Saints ball cap, was bent over, looking through the driver's side window; number two, wearing a Dallas Cowboys cap, stood watch on the opposite side of the vehicle. Cowboy Cap spotted Jack approaching the car.

"Oh, man! Here he comes," he said to Saints Cap.

Saints Cap looked up quickly and spotted Jack approaching the Camaro. "This here ride yours, mister?" he asked. "Shore is a nice one—1978, '79? I bet she's got a V8 with a four-barrel quad-carburetor—350 cubic inch, right, mister?"

"I didn't know looking through the window could tell you so much about the engine," Jack said.

"Yeah, well, we was just checkin' out the color of the interior," Saints Cap replied. "I see it's all black inside. Shoot man, it must git awful hot come summertime."

"Just move away from the car," Jack commanded.

He waited for them to make their move, and wasn't surprised when they did. Nor was he disappointed. Saints Cap began walking toward him first. Cowboy Cap headed toward him, as well, but a little more reluctance showed in his step. Jack's eyes missed nothing. Cowboy Cap was solid and stocky, but it was Saints Cap who concerned Jack the most. Saints Cap's rapid approach and wiry frame alerted Jack he'd have to be dealt with first. Cowboy Cap began to falter and he held back momentarily, but soon quickened his pace as he watched Saints Cap move steadily and rapidly toward Jack.

Jack placed his bags on the pavement, a foot or so away from his left foot, and readied himself for their approach. He set his stance: left leg slightly forward, right slightly back. Perfectly balanced. Ready. He closed his fists and held them in front of his chest, ready to strike.

"Hey, Randy," Cowboy Cap suddenly blurted out. "I don't think we need to be messin' with this one. He looks like he knows what he's doin'."

Randy halted his approach, and without turning he spoke to Cowboy Cap. "Shoot, Billy. I ain't afraid of this guy," he replied. "Just 'cause he stands there lookin' like Kwai Chang Caine don't mean nothin'. I done beat one of these tae kwon do heads before and I can prob-ly take this one, too."

Jack smiled. *Come and get me, you idiot.*

"Randy, I think you better listen to me this time," Billy said. "He don't look like that other fella. He looks like he knows what he's doin'. What style karate is that, mister?"

Jack never took his eyes off Randy as he replied, "That's for you and your buddy to find out, isn't it?"

Billy walked up to Randy and grabbed him with both hands. "Randy, let's go," he said. "This ain't worth it."

Randy shrugged Billy away. He glared at Jack, but something must have clicked in his brain; his aggressiveness slowly subsided. Jack kept his gaze fixed on him, nonetheless.

"Shoot, mister," Randy said, finally breaking the silence. "We was just admirin' your wheels. No real harm in that, is there?"

When Jack said nothing in reply, Randy and Billy turned and walked toward the entrance. Jack watched them until they entered the restaurant. He picked up his bags and backed toward his car, keeping his eyes on the entrance. He knew the type, and figured the wiry one—the one named Randy—might just change his mind and come back out and head toward him again. He put the key in the door lock and continued to watch, and through the window he could see the other—Billy—talking to Randy, who was staring back through the glass at Jack. Billy's actions were quite animated, and Jack figured Billy was trying to talk some sense into the younger Randy. Jack got in his car, placed the two bags on the front floorboard on the passenger side, reached over, unlocked the glove compartment, and pulled out the .45 and placed it on his lap. He started the engine, shifted into reverse, and backed out of the parking space. He smiled when he spotted Randy coming out the front door of the Burger King, heading straight toward him. *You idiot*, he thought as he shifted into park, rolled the window down, pulled the slide back on the .45, and aimed the barrel at Randy's chest. Randy came to an abrupt stop when he saw the gun in Jack's right hand.

"Randy, I think it's best if you turn around and go back inside. Billy's right, you know. There are some people in this world you just don't mess with. I'm one of them."

Billy came out of the lobby of the Burger King, grabbed Randy, and pulled him toward him and the lobby door. "You stupid fool!" he said. "What would I go and tell Mama if that man blowed a hole in you? Randy, that's a Colt .45 he pulled on you! Like the one Daddy carried with him in Korea. He coulda killed you!" Billy paused, then added, "Maybe I shoulda let him just kick your rear end all over this parkin' lot, but that woulda done no good. You woulda kept on anyway until you got him to pull that gun on you, even after he kicked your butt good. Man, little brother! When you ever gonna learn?"

Jack continued to watch Billy yell at Randy and waited for him to pull his little brother back into the restaurant. He placed the .45 back on his lap, shifted back into Drive, and pulled around the building to the exit sign. He made a right turn, back onto the highway, crossed back under the interstate, and turned left onto the westbound entrance ramp. He pulled to the right shoulder of the ramp, opened the glove compartment, and placed the .45 back in it and closed the door. He let off the brake and pressed the accelerator and the Camaro lurched forward once again, gathering speed along the ramp to merge with the flow of traffic headed west on the interstate.

Jack soon spotted the first of the two green Biloxi exit signs and had just driven past it when he saw another green sign ahead and to the right shoulder of the interstate. He read the information he was most interested in: "New Orleans 90." He calculated it would take just under an hour and a half to reach the eastern edge of the city. He began to think about the rest of the plan. Another half hour or so to negotiate his way through the downtown streets. Pay and leave the Camaro at a parking deck on St. Charles. Walk over to Canal Street and hail a taxi to the Hertz location at the airport. Pick up a rental there under one of his assumed identities and drive to the Monteleone on Royal Street in the French Quarter. It would be a late evening, but that would be okay. The Carousel Bar would be open, and a couple of drinks would be a good way to end the day. Plus, he knew he'd have had a very comfortable bed waiting for him at the hotel. If the demons stayed away he might get a good night's sleep tonight. All part of the plan. He thought of a familiar phrase: *If you fail to plan, you plan to fail.* He hadn't failed yet. He wasn't about to start now.

***

The adrenaline that had kicked in back in the Burger King parking lot had subsided now, and the pang of hunger returned. He reached over and picked up the two carry-out bags and placed them on the passenger seat next to him. He opened the food bag, found the fry container, and pulled it out and ate all of the fries before he extracted the Whopper. He unwrapped it and held it in his left hand. He quickly finished it and then reached into the drink bag and pulled out the Coke first. Three long sips and it was gone. *Now for the chocolate shake*, he thought. He removed the wrapper on another straw, inserted it into the lid of the shake, and took a long sip. The shake had warmed a little and was slightly melted, but there was no harm in that in Jack's mind. It was a darn good chocolate shake. He pictured the little boy and his father in his mind and smiled. *Dad was just like him*, Jack thought. *Hovering over us, smiling in delight at the little things we did. Man, I sure do miss him.*

He set the empty bags on the front floorboard, intending to dispose of them when he stopped and found a trash can. He often watched people throw their trash out the window on the highway, but he wasn't one of them. Just one of those pet peeves of his, seeing people do that; it made him want to chase them down, pull his gun out, and shoot at them.

At least shake them up, he thought. *Can't shoot everybody, even though some of them deserve it. Like Randy back there. I could have, maybe should have, but there was nothing to be gained by it.* "Let it go, Jack," he told himself aloud. "Let it go."

He gently eased down on the accelerator and watched the needle on the speedometer rise to sixty, and he held it there. He pressed the ZZ Top cassette back into the player on the dash and found "LaGrange" for the umpteenth time. He cranked up the volume, made himself a little more comfortable in his seat, and began bobbing to the beat of the music. The sun was sinking quickly in the western sky, painting the adjacent low-lying clouds purple and pink and red. He watched the orange ball drop lower and lower in the sky, and knew he'd be in the Big Easy not long after dark. That was fine with him. Entering the city at night listening to ZZ Top. *Life is good*, he concluded. *It just doesn't get any better than this.*

CHAPTER 4

The next morning Jack sat at one of the outer tables at the Café du Monde while he waited for his order of café au lait and beignets to arrive. It was only ten o'clock, and already the temperature had climbed to 80. It was headed higher. Earlier that morning, he had turned on the television set in his hotel room to catch the local news and the weather report.

"Sunny, with a high today of 92," the meteorologist on the news show had reported. "The humidity level will be in the double digits, up around eighty percent," he also added.

Jack agreed with the rest of the forecaster's comments on Channel 2's morning show; both the temperature and the humidity *were* running higher than usual for this time of year. This late-April morning was beginning to feel more like an early summer one due to the combination of these two factors. He'd often heard it said they were the city's only real faults.

But Jack loved New Orleans enough to overlook any of its faults. He knew the best time to come was between October and March, when it was milder and more pleasant. Occasionally it got downright cold in the middle of that stretch, but those months were certainly more bearable than the rest of the year. And Mardi Gras, a can't-miss event if ever there was one, beckoned him during that time. The rest of the year, however hot and sticky it was bound to get, came with the territory. He and every other warm-weather visitor to the city had no choice but to grin and bear it when it came to the heat and humidity that just seemed to wrap itself around everything and everyone.

Jack Brantley had long ago resolved to come to New Orleans as often as he could, whether for business or pleasure—or a combination of the two, such as now. He often wished he had the luxury of coming and going when he wanted, but he knew that was impossible. His clients' wishes came first, and he was paid quite well for taking care of those wishes. They weren't paying him to fulfill *his* needs and desires; they were paying him in cash—lots of it—to fulfill *theirs*. He was okay with that, as long as the price was right. And so he found himself here, on a gorgeous late-spring morning. Though it was getting a little too close to his discomfort level, he was grateful he wasn't smack-dab in the middle of a hot New Orleans summer.

The waiter arrived with Jack's order and placed a steaming cup of café au lait and a plate laden with three beignets on the tiny table. He placed a glass of ice water, a spoon, and several napkins on the table along with the check. Jack reached for his wallet, pulled out a ten, and handed it to the waiter.

"I'll be right back with your change, sir," the waiter said as he departed.

Jack reached for one of the powder-covered doughnuts, picked it up, and bit into it. *God, that tastes so good*, he thought. He quickly finished it, then picked up the ceramic cup and took a sip of the hot, rich, dark coffee that had been mixed with scalded milk. The Café du Monde never failed to delight his palate. It was one of his favorite haunts in the Quarter, and he never failed to visit it each time he came to New Orleans.

Jack was finishing the last of the beignets when the waiter returned and placed the change from the ten on the table.

"Thank you, sir," the waiter said. "My name is Rafael. Is there anything else I can get for you?"

"Actually, there is, Rafael," Jack replied. "Would you bring me another cup, a large one, please?"

"Certainly, sir," Rafael said. "Would you like another order of beignets, as well?"

"I'd like to, but I can't. Those three were my limit. What I'd really love is that second cup of coffee, and I'd like to just sit here a while and drink it and enjoy the view. You don't mind if I do that, do you? I have some time to kill."

"I have to say that I agree with you," Rafael replied. "The café certainly has a unique vantage point for people watching," he added. "We're not terribly busy, so please take your time. I will return with your order momentarily."

Jack picked up the first cup of coffee and sipped from it, finishing it just as Rafael returned with the second cup and placed it on the table with the check. Jack handed Rafael another ten-dollar bill.

"You have some change coming, sir. I'll be back in a moment," Rafael said.

"That's not necessary," Jack replied. "That's to cover the coffee. Whatever's left is for you, my friend."

"Thank you *very* much sir," Rafael said as he removed the cup and saucer from the first order and the empty beignet plate, as well. "Please enjoy. And take all the time you need. Shall I check back with you for anything else?"

"No," Jack replied. "This will be all, thank you."

"Then it has been a pleasure to have served you, sir," Rafael said as he turned and walked away.

Jack directed his attention to the street in front of him and began watching the growing parade of tourists and locals passing by. The crowd was beginning to swell on Decatur Street now; he knew that by noon, or shortly thereafter, the café would be filled, as well. But that was another hour and a half away. Plenty of time. He did not need to be in the Warehouse/Arts District until early afternoon, and he had the rest of the morning to do what he wanted. And what he wanted right now was to sit, relax, and enjoy the second cup and just watch who, and sometimes what, went by. It was a hobby of his, a way to unwind and de-stress, and he particularly enjoyed it here in the French Quarter. He read somewhere New Orleans had been labeled "America's Most Interesting City." It certainly was, based on the interesting characters parading by in front of him. His personal favorite was "the Big Easy." *So easy on the senses,* he thought.

Jack *did* take his time to finish the second cup of coffee. He was tempted to get Rafael's attention once more, to throw caution to the wind and order a third cup, but he knew that would add far too much caffeine to his system and he'd pay for it later in the day. He reached for his wallet again, extracted a five-dollar bill, and laid it on the table. He knew from past observations when he dined here that far too many of the tourists flocking to the café left little or nothing for their waiters. It always appalled him when he saw it taking place and he tried to make up for the shortfall when he was here. He hoped the locals felt the same way and did likewise. *A little something extra, Rafael. You guys work way too hard to get stiffed like that.*

He got up and crossed Decatur and entered Jackson Square to see the local artists and street performers at work. He wanted to stroll along its sidewalks and watch them, and then continue from there on the short walk back to his hotel on Royal Street. He had walked from the Monteleone to the Café du Monde this morning for the fresh air and exercise, and planned to walk back by the same route.

It was getting hotter as it grew closer and closer to noon. Jack knew he could hail a taxi and return in its air-conditioned comfort, but he decided to endure the rising temperature and humidity level and finish the walk instead, and enjoy more of the Quarter.

As he meandered through the crowded square he did a mental run-through of the general plans he had for the rest of the day. First, he would return to the hotel and have the valet retrieve his rental car from the hotel's parking deck. From there he planned to drive into the Warehouse/Arts District of the city and locate the man he had been hired to kill. He had laid out his plans for the job quite carefully—he had examined the recent photos he requested, he was quite familiar with the major streets he'd need to negotiate, he had the address where the target could be found this afternoon, and he had familiarized himself with the routines and habits of the target.

When he first learned of the name and occupation of the intended hit, he thought it was a bit unusual for his client to go to such lengths, and expense, to have the man taken out, but he dismissed it rather quickly. A job was a job, and this was no different from the others. A job to be done, and it paid well. He was obligated to his client to get it done, and it was none of his business why it was to be done. The fee for doing so went a long way in erasing any doubts or concerns he might have; fees had a special way of doing that.

The final part of the day's plan was where it got a little tricky, but he knew he'd manage through it. After the job was done, he would find a spot to ditch the rental—perhaps near the lakeshore—and hail a taxi to take him to the parking deck on St. Charles where he had left his Camaro. Leaving from there he would simply drive into the French Quarter, free and unencumbered to do what he wanted there. He had no other obligations, no assignments, no contracts, nothing on his schedule for the next few days, so he planned to enjoy the many pleasures the *Vieux Carre* had to offer.

One of the things he looked forward to most was the downtime. Time to join in and do what the natives were doing: enjoying life. It was what he loved *most* about the city—their attitude about life. And about time. He loved the laid-back nature of the people who lived and worked in this city, and especially those in the Quarter. Schedules and agendas and deadlines didn't matter so much to them. There seemed to be an endless supply of time for these people to enjoy the things life had to offer. He long ago adopted the city's unofficial saying as his own when he came here. He still had trouble with his French, and he wished it would roll off his tongue as someone fluent in the language would say it. "*Nous ne sommes pas presses*," he said aloud and as best he could but to no one in particular.

He walked farther along the sidewalk, to the center of the park, and approached the statue that dominated its center. Andrew Jackson sat high, mounted on his horse, hat in hand, gazing off into the distance, as if he had something of importance on his mind and somewhere he had to be. Jack thought back to his American history class in high school and what he had learned in that class about the man. What he remembered most was that the general was a hot-tempered, impatient man who was obsessed with his future and his place in the country's politics. Quite suitable for Washington, but not here in New Orleans. Not even back then. *He's probably looking for the nearest exit out of here*, Jack thought.

As he walked around the statue on his way out of the square, Jack gently chided the general for his impatience and preoccupation with matters other than New Orleans.

"Remember what they say, General," Jack whispered in passing, "*nous ne sommes pas presses.* No rush. No hurry."

CHAPTER 5

After leaving Jackson Square on its north side, opposite the St. Louis Cathedral, Jack turned left and walked along Chartres Street. He took his time strolling down Chartres, and when he reached Bienville Street he turned right. He leisurely walked the next two blocks, window-shopping, people watching, and when he reached the intersection with Royal Street he turned left and arrived back at the Monteleone. The heat and humidity during the stroll to the Café du Monde and the return walk back to the hotel had made him sweat profusely; he felt clammy and in dire need of a shower and a new set of clothes. He entered the lobby and walked through the cool, softly lit interior of the hotel to an elevator, rode up to the third floor, quickly exited, and walked down the hall to his room.

***

After he toweled himself dry and finished in the bathroom he walked over to the closet. He pulled out a crisp white dress shirt, freshly ironed tan slacks, a dark-brown dress belt, a navy-blue blazer, and a green-and-navy-blue striped tie that were hanging in the closet. He picked up the dark-brown leather dress shoes from the floor of the closet, walked over to the bed, laid out the clothes on the bed and shoes on the floor, and stepped back to examine them. He glanced over at the closet, and looked at the three-hundred-dollar light-grey suit that hung there, but decided against wearing it after all. The suit would be too over the top for today.

Sure would look good on me, though, he thought. He looked back at the clothing lying on the bed. *This will have to do.* He reassured himself, finally concluding, *It's all good. Still professional looking. More in line with what an insurance salesman or a legal assistant at a law firm could afford.*

When he had finished dressing, Jack walked over to the chest of drawers, opened the top drawer, and extracted the shoulder holster and the .45 automatic. He strapped on the shoulder harness, placed the .45 in the holster, and walked back over to the bed. He put on the jacket and turned to check himself in the full-length mirror hanging next to the closet door. He placed an extra clip for the .45 in the left outer pocket of the blazer, gathered his wallet and keys to the rental car from the top of the dresser, and placed them in his pant pockets. He went over to the bed, picked up the briefcase that sat on the floor next to the bed, and turned toward the door. He walked out of the hotel room and pulled the door behind him. He hung the DO NOT DISTURB sign on the outer handle, and checked the door handle.

Good, he thought. *Locked. Everything's secure.* He reached for the handle again, to check it once more, to be absolutely certain, but forced himself to stop. He knew going through with it, checking it again, would only reinforce what that army shrink also wrote in that damn report of his years ago. Jack had memorized the report, word for word, and what he focused on now was the part he hated.

. . .Furthermore, Specialist 4 John Thomas Brantley exhibits a condition known as obsessive-compulsive disorder. From my interviews, observations, and assessment of Specialist Brantley, I have concluded that, while this condition would be unlikely to be detrimental to him and others in his company, his condition could lead to further complications and problems. . . Blah, blah, blah.

He went so far as to consider removing the sign from the door. There was no real need for it, as room service was through for the day and no one else would enter the room. He chastised himself. *Quit being so careful and so paranoid, Jack.* Then he thought of one of his rules, and he left the sign in place.

"Better to err on the side of caution," he said aloud as he walked toward the elevator.

***

Jack stood outside the front entrance of the Monteleone, waiting patiently for the young valet to retrieve his rental car from the hotel's parking deck. While he waited he struck up a conversation with the doorman.

"I hope you've been enjoying your stay with us, Mr. Pittman," the doorman said. "Have you had a chance to spend any time in the Quarter yet?"

"I hope to be able to do just that this evening, my friend," Jack replied. "This is only my second time visiting your wonderful city. I didn't have much time when I was here last, so I'm going to make up for the missed opportunities. I hope to find a great restaurant tonight. I hear there are so many to choose from. After I wrap up all these darn meetings this afternoon, I've got the evening to myself. Got any recommendations?"

Jack was lying, of course. He had a nearly encyclopedic knowledge of the French Quarter and its restaurants, its bars, and its lounges. But he was here under the name of Richard Pittman of Houston, Texas. A mid-level executive who worked for the Shell Oil Company. In town for a couple of days, he was passing himself off as a very busy man with important meetings to attend each afternoon. He was using this guise for only the second time; this hit involved a much more public figure in the city, not some obscure resident of Nowhere, Alabama, as was the last job. He made the decision to be *very* cautious. Another rule to operate by came to mind. Something he carried over from his school days. *Better safe than sorry,* he thought. There was always the danger of his cover being blown, of some misstep occurring. Not that it should happen, but it could. He had other covers for future jobs, such as Robert Tilton. But Tilton was from New Orleans, so he chose not to use that cover here. Too risky. He would save it and use it again somewhere else. If a newer, fresher cover was required, he knew he could count on Eddie Trask to come up with one, along with the necessary, carefully crafted documents. But for now, he would pose as Richard Pittman, and he'd let the doorman and the young valet remain under the impression that he was from out of town and, as someone unfamiliar with New Orleans, a guy who could really use the recommendations.

From his casual observations, Jack knew the valet was pretty young, and therefore probably inexperienced in the subtleties and nuances of the Quarter. He thought the doorman was much older, probably as old, if not older, than himself. The valet probably hadn't hit his twenty-first birthday in stride yet. If he surpassed the mark, then good for him; if not, Jack wished him Godspeed.

He turned his attention to the older fellow standing beside him. Why not strike up a conversation? Pick his brain about the Quarter. At the very least, kill a few minutes while waiting for the car to arrive. His previous encounters with the doorman so far—last night, and again this morning—were positive ones for Jack. *He certainly seems enthusiastic about the job*, Jack thought. *One of those eager-to-please types, I'll bet.* Jack hoped the man did have some good experiences in the Quarter to talk about. *It'll be my luck the guy's a teetotaler.* He was looking for something different tonight, someplace he hadn't been before, and could use a local's take on it. A great recommendation was what was required. *Let's fish for one.*

Jack had already made his decision where he wanted to eat tonight— there was no better place than Galatoire's. If there were, he didn't know about it. He planned to dine alone there, to savor the meal and the ambience. To enjoy the whole experience of the place again, without the added burden of carrying on a conversation with someone he really didn't want to be with in the first place. It was okay to be alone; not always, of course, but he chose to be alone often.

During his tenure with the CIA, Jack Brantley had been branded as a "lone wolf" and, unlike others who had been stamped the same, he didn't mind that label at all. After all, it *was* true. He needed people only to fulfill his purposes. A woman was, as far as he was concerned, designed to satisfy a particular need. It wasn't for conversation. More than one woman tried to get close to him, but he maintained his distance and chose to live and work alone.

Jack knew he'd have plenty of time, once the job was finished, to satisfy his palate at Galatoire's. What he was looking for was a new place to pick up a woman to satisfy another need. Someplace that was a little different or unusual had to exist in the Quarter; he just had to find it or be made aware of its existence. He needed to keep from getting completely bored playing the same tiresome game. He knew how to play it, of course, and picking up a woman at a bar was far more challenging, and ultimately more satisfying, than paying for a hooker. He had plenty of money for them, and he found some of them to be true professionals plying their trade. Paying for a woman was the last option for him, and he was hoping it would not end up that way in the Quarter tonight.

He decided to see what places the doorman knew of and would recommend. He was even willing to wager on the outcome. *It's up to you, bud*, he thought. *Point me in the direction of some wild women. Your tip's riding on the outcome.*

He thought back to a previous interaction he'd had with a doorman at a hotel in downtown Jacksonville. He remembered he knew little of the city's nightlife, and the doorman there came through admirably. *Let's see how this one does.* He set the scale for judging today's recommendation. *Average and predictable, just a five*, Jack thought. *Above average, but still predictable, a ten. Superior, someplace I've never been or just have to check out the babes, a twenty.* He was curious to see how it would play out with this man.

"Well, sir, you can't go wrong if you were to choose to dine at Galatoire's," the doorman answered when asked which restaurant to eat at. "Their Oysters Rockefeller and Shrimp Amandine come highly recommended."

Agreeable. So far so good, Jack thought. *At least a ten coming your way.*

"And then afterward, there's no better place than Pat O'Brien's. The Hurricane they serve there is a must for anyone visiting New Orleans. . ."

Oops, you're slipping, Jack thought. *Been there. Done that. Minus five for the faux pas.*

"...and if you're into Jazz, then there's no better place to hear it than at the Preservation Hall. I'll be glad to give you directions to any of them, if you'd like."

So far, just average, Jack thought. *Come on, man, you can do better than that. Earn your money, for God's sake!*

Jack assumed the doorman, like so many doormen and concierges and valets, was well-trained by his supervisor or some other staff member of the Monteleone to recommend the usual tourist stops. *Maybe they have a special training session for it,* he thought. *Titled something like "Places of Interest to Tell Visitors When They Bother to Ask."* He wanted to see how much this guy *really* knew about the Big Easy. Jack had been to all of them on numerous occasions, and though they were fine, greater places beckoned.

Jack looked at the name tag he was wearing. "Well, Andrew, I have heard of Galatoire's, and because you're recommending it, then Galatoire's it is," he said. "For the food, of course. But what I need is something more than Pat O'Brien's. Not that there's anything wrong with it. It's just that I was there the last time I visited the city. I need a bar or lounge with a little more local flavor to it." Jack looked at the name again. "So tell me, Andrew. What's another place I could go to?"

"Then you've gotta go to Donna's, over on Rampart Street," Andrew replied. "Too bad you're gonna eat at Galatoire's, Mr. Pittman. The barbeque and the red beans and rice Donna's serves is as good as you can get, both for the flavor of New Orleans and for the money. The drinks are okay, kinda average. But you gotta check out the brass bands that play there. Their music is first rate."

Better, Jack thought. *You're up to a ten again, bubba. Let's see if you've got an ace up your sleeve.* "Come on, Andrew," he said aloud. "Between you and me—I know we just met and don't know one another—but level with me. In your personal opinion, where's the real action? I'm looking for a good time tonight. A real good time, if you know what I mean."

"I tell you, Mr. Pittman, I really don't hit the bars like I used to," Andrew replied. "Don't play the field much anymore, either, not since I met up with a special lady. Her name's Belinda, and she don't like to go out much. We stay in a lot during the week. Go out Friday or Saturday nights, depending on which one I get as my night off. That's about it. So I guess I'm not much good to you, for that kind of advice, I mean."

"Ah, that's all right, Andrew," Jack said. "I'll just stumble my way around the Quarter tonight. Maybe I'll get lucky anyway."

Jack turned his attention back to the activity on the street, watching for the arrival of his rented Oldsmobile Cutlass. This part of Royal Street was designated one way, east to west. He looked to the right and spotted the silver car rolling slowly toward the front of the hotel. When it pulled alongside the front, the doorman turned to Jack and spoke again.

"Mr. Pittman, if I may say so, I think I know who may have an answer for you. Bobby's about to get out of your car and maybe he can point you in the right direction."

"Who, *him*? The one who went to get my car? He's just a kid," Jack said.

"You'd be surprised," Andrew said. "I know he looks like he's fresh outta high school and all. But he's actually twenty-two, about to turn twenty-three this summer."

"You can't be serious," Jack replied.

"As a heart attack, Mr. Pittman," Andrew said. "Go ahead and ask him. Lots of folks don't believe it, either. Ask him to show you his driver's license. He won't mind if you do. He's used to people not believing how old he is, so when push comes to shove, if they still don't believe him, he pulls out the license without them even asking. Just to prove it. He has a bit of a chip on his shoulder, I think."

"I just may take you up on that, Andrew," Jack said as he pulled out a ten-dollar bill from his pants pocket and handed it to the doorman. "See ya' around."

"Thank you, Mr. Pittman," Andrew said. "Don't know if I did much to deserve it, but thank you very much."

"You suggested Galatoire's to me, and Donna's," Jack stated. "And I enjoyed talkin' to you."

Jack walked over to the rental. Bobby was standing beside the left front door and held it open for him. Jack handed him the briefcase, and Bobby leaned into the car and placed it on the front passenger seat. He stood up, and stepped aside so that Jack could gain access to the vehicle.

"Young man," Jack began, "Andrew over there tells me your name is Bobby, and from what I'm told you may have some experience in the Quarter. That you might be able to point me in the direction of someplace unusual. I already know about O'Brien's and Donna's, the Preservation Hall, all the usual tourist stops. So what's someplace you'd recommend? A personal favorite?"

Jack decided he'd use the same criteria he applied to Andrew. *Come on, kid, your tip's riding on this*, he thought.

"You ain't gonna be like them others, Mr. Pittman, and think I'm too young for the Quarter?" Bobby asked. "I get so tired of people thinkin' I ain't even out of high school yet."

"No, Bobby," Jack replied. "No need to go there. I have to admit you do look young, but Andrew over there vouches for you. Says you've been around some. What I'm hoping is you've found a place where the locals hang out. I know I'm from out of town but I do like to catch some of the local flavor. A place with good drinks and music, but more importantly with good-looking women who are looking for a good time."

"Mr. Pittman, since you asked, I'll be glad to tell you. There ain't nothing in the Quarter quite like the Famous Door over on Bourbon Street," Andrew replied. "It totally rocks, if you know what I mean. And the women there! Ain't none easier to pick up, in my opinion and experience." He seemed embarrassed when he said it, and then added, "If that's what you have in mind, Mr. Pittman."

Bingo, kid! Jack thought. *You just earned yourself a twenty.* "I just may take you up on your advice, Bobby. Andrew has recommended Galatoire's for my dinner and I think I'll stick with that. Afterward, I may just wander on over to Bourbon Street and pay a visit to this Famous Door place that you so highly recommend. Thanks again. Here's a little something, just for leveling with me," he said aloud as he winked and handed Bobby a twenty-dollar bill.

"Thank you," Bobby said as he examined it. "Man, that's awesome. I hope you have a good afternoon, Mr. Pittman. And an even better evening, wherever it takes you. If it's to the Famous Door, I just may see you there."

That's a possibility, Jack thought. *Kid, if I score while I'm there, I'll buy you a drink. If she's hot, I'll pick up your tab for the whole night.*

***

Jack left the Monteleone, headed west on Royal, and quickly came to the intersection at Canal Street. It was early afternoon, and the traffic on Canal in both directions was thick and slow moving. He had expected it to be and was not disappointed in his prediction. He heard it said—more than a few times—that Canal was arguably the most heavily used north-and-south route in the downtown area, and it was true. It certainly was at this time of the day. In his opinion, it was always busy, no matter what time it was.

Jack waited patiently for the light to turn green and the traffic to clear the intersection before he chanced crossing the busy street. Once through the intersection the road became St. Charles Avenue, and Jack continued driving west on the crowded street, alongside the street's infamous green-colored streetcars. He glanced over as they passed by, each one heavily laden with tourists and locals alike. The cars ran on tracks in the middle of the street and were headed west out of the Business District to pass through the Warehouse/Arts District and into the western end of the city with its fine homes in the Garden District.

Jack inched the Cutlass along the busy confines of St. Charles; several minutes later he passed through the intersection at Poydras Street. Not as familiar with the cross streets as wished he were, he began looking for Julia Street. After a couple of blocks he found it and turned right onto it and followed Julia northward; two blocks later he saw the street sign indicating he was at the intersection of Julia and Baronne. He made a left turn onto Baronne and saw the building housing the Catholic Charities office, just ahead and on his right. He drove slowly along Baronne, and stopped in front of the building. He glanced out the right front window and read the sign that stood between the sidewalk and the front of the building.

CATHOLIC CHARITIES OFFICE

ARCHDIOCESE OF NEW ORLEANS

825 BARONNE STREET

According to the information provided to him from his client, Jack should find his intended target here this afternoon. He drove a little farther along the street until he spotted an empty parking space on the right side at the end of the block. He pulled into the space, leaving the engine running. He reached over and opened the briefcase he had placed on the front seat next to him. He pulled out the intel report and read it again:

Father Edward Brennan. Age forty-five. Height: six-one. Weight: one seventy-five to one eighty. Thin, light-brown hair, receding hairline. No visible scars. Assigned to the Catholic Charities Office, 825 Baronne Street, New Orleans (Warehouse/Arts District), Monday through Friday, 1 p.m. to 5 p.m. Otherwise, subject can be found at various times performing his duties as associate parish priest at the Sacred Heart of Jesus Catholic Church, 7067 St. Charles Ave., New Orleans (Garden District, near Loyola University). Subject resides at the rectory behind the church building. Subject says Mass at the church every Saturday at 5 p.m. and every Sunday at 8 a.m. Extremely busy area. Unless absolutely necessary, I suggest making no contact with subject at the church, its adjacent office, or the residence building. Recommend contact be made with subject at the Catholic Charities Office on Baronne St. Tuesday or Wednesday. Thursday if necessary. Fewer clientele has been observed those afternoons. Definitely avoid contact Monday and Friday. Streets around office are

extremely busy then with vehicular traffic, and foot traffic going into and
exiting the office is heavy those afternoons.

Jack had read the intel report a couple of times prior to this, and now
for the third time, sitting in the Cutlass at the end of the block. The surveillance man was obviously a pro and, from what Jack could tell just by
reading the report, appeared to have his act together. However, what Jack
found most interesting each time he read the report was a handwritten
note the surveillance man enclosed with the report. Jack heard his client
had objected, but the man insisted on its inclusion.

Personal notes and observations:

Subject is rarely seen by himself. Subject is very engaging and appears
to enjoy having lots of people around him. It may be difficult to find
him alone during normal business hours. After hours may be the best
approach. I did approach the subject once at the church, on the pretense
of being lost and needing directions. Subject invited me into his office
and asked me about my family, church attendance, other things of a
personal nature. Said he was from St. Louis, that his mother had been
sick. Asked if he could pray for me and my family. I declined, but he was
persistent, and he prayed anyway. Unusual man, to say the least. Hope
this helps when the time comes.

Well, well, Father Edward Brennan, Jack thought. *Looks like you're one*
of those "touchy-feely" types. A "people" kind of guy.

As he glanced at the handwritten note again, Jack was reminded of
Father De Marco back home in Pensacola, at St. Michael's Church downtown. If he wasn't at the church he was at the school up on the hill on
Palafox Street, visiting the classrooms and sharing the mysteries of the
Catholic faith. *What a talker!* Jack remembered. He looked once again at
the photo of Father Brennan, then he placed the report and photo inside
the briefcase and closed it.

Bless me, Father, I'm about to sin, he thought.

CHAPTER 6

Jack turned off the engine to the Cutlass, opened the front door and stepped out. He immediately felt the afternoon heat, and was certain the temperature had made it to the predicted high of 92 for the day. *May have made it to 95, from the way it feels right now*, he thought. *Must be this god-awful humidity making it feel hotter.*

He felt himself starting to sweat already under the blue blazer; he couldn't chance taking it off as he was still wearing the shoulder harness and carrying the .45 in the holster underneath his jacket. He closed the door and checked his appearance in the glass. He had loosened the tie and had left his collar unbuttoned until now; he quickly re-buttoned the shirt collar and pulled the knot of the tie tighter. He walked around to the right front door, opened it, and extracted the briefcase from the front seat, pressed the AUTOMATIC LOCK button to secure all the doors to the vehicle, and turned to walk up the short sidewalk to the building.

Jack was carrying the briefcase securely in his left hand when he opened the front door and walked through it into the Catholic Charities Office. He immediately noticed how cool it was inside. Cold, actually. There was no doubt it was hot outside and the office staff had to run the A/C, but running it so low this early in the year. . . *Wow, the Archdiocese's gonna hate to see this month's electric bill*, he thought. *They keep this up in here and somebody's gonna flip out when they have to pay the bill.*

Attempting to locate the receptionist, Jack looked to his left, didn't see anyone, and turned to his right. He spotted an attractive, middle-aged black woman wearing a light-pink blouse. She was seated behind a desk that sat perpendicular to the front door. Jack wondered why the desk was off to the side like that, instead of right in front of the door as most offices were set up. Missing little, his eyes found the answer. He looked at the ceiling and saw that she sat under an overhead A/C vent; that vent was blasting cold air into the room and she was the initial recipient of its cooling effects. He noticed the pink blouse she was wearing was short-sleeved and made of a thin material, and wondered how she could function in such a cold room.

Jack noticed she was on the phone and, although he hated to invade her privacy, he walked toward her desk anyway. She was speaking at the time when she looked up at Jack as he approached her. She cupped her hand over the phone and said to him, "I'll be with you in a moment, sir." She then removed her hand and spoke again into the receiver. Jack stood quietly in front of her desk and listened.

"That's right, Mrs. Sanders. You can come here today if you'd like, and I'll be glad to assist you with the forms, but as I said, Father Brennan won't be here today to speak with you personally. He's away for the afternoon. His former housekeeper's son died and he's with her and her family right now. He assured me he'll be in tomorrow. You're welcome to try back then."

Jack glanced at the sign that sat on her desk. Bernice Abernathy. He continued waiting as Bernice spoke into the phone again.

"I don't know how it happened, Mrs. Sanders. I just know Father Brennan called from his office at the church this morning and told me he wouldn't be in this afternoon. He told me the young man was dead but he wouldn't give me any details. He just said for me to tell anyone who asked that he would be here tomorrow afternoon."

Another minute, maybe two, ticked by. Bernice was silent, obviously listening to Mrs. Sanders ramble some more. Jack began drumming his fingers on his briefcase. Bernice looked up and winked at Jack as she spoke into the phone again. "I *do* understand your situation, Mrs. Sanders. Believe me, I do. . . Yes, ma'am, I'll make sure Father Brennan sees you tomorrow. . . At two. . . Yes, ma'am. I'm putting you down on his schedule. He will speak with you privately in his office just as you request. Good-bye, Mrs. Sanders."

Jack watched as Bernice finished penciling in the appointment on the calendar that sat on her desk. She hung up the phone and looked up at Jack again. He was no longer drumming his fingers on the briefcase.

"Now, how may I help you, sir?" she asked.

Jack looked down at the nameplate again on the desk. "Well. . . Mrs.? Miss? Abernathy. . ." Jack said. "May I call you Bernice?"

"It's Mrs. Abernathy when I'm here, Mr.. . .? I'm sorry. I didn't get your name, sir."

"Richard Pittman, ma'am," Jack said as he reached into his shirt pocket and extracted a business card. "Richard Pittman, with the Northern Gulf Coast Life Insurance Company of Baton Rouge." Jack handed Bernice one of the business cards Eddie had created for him.

Bernice inspected the card, then placed it on her desk pad in front of her. "How may I help you, Mr. Pittman?"

"You can call me Richard," Jack said.

"I'd prefer to keep it businesslike, sir. So, Mr. Pittman, how may I help you today?"

"Well, Mrs. Abernathy, I had hoped to meet with Father Brennan this afternoon," Jack said. "But according to what I just heard—I'm sorry, I didn't mean to eavesdrop—I don't think that's going to happen now, is it? And I came here, all the way from Baton Rouge to meet with him."

"Did you have an appointment with Father Brennan?" she asked while looking at the calendar on her desk. A few seconds later she looked up at Jack. He noticed a slight smile was beginning to form on her face. "I see that your name doesn't appear on his appointment calendar for today, Mr. Pittman."

"No, ma'am, I didn't have an appointment. I was told yesterday by someone at the archdiocese office that it wouldn't be a problem to drop by and catch him here this afternoon. You see, I have Father Brennan's new policy with me and I wanted to deliver it to him personally. He has to sign it for it to be in force."

"Well, Mr. Pittman, as you have heard, his former housekeeper's son is dead, and he won't be in until tomorrow afternoon."

"Yes, ma'am, and I'm so sorry to hear that. You said you don't know any of the details. I do hope the boy's mama had him insured and all. You never know when a tragedy will occur and take a loved one away. The cost of funerals these days, well. . . Oh, I'm so sorry. There I go again. I bet you think I'm terrible, what with the boy's sudden demise and all, but I just can't get the life insurance side of me to ever shut up."

To Jack, the initial hostility in Bernice's voice seemed to have faded away, and her demeanor changed, as well. "That's all right, Mr. Pittman," she said. "I'm sorry you've missed Father Brennan on what seems to be to be an important personal matter for him. I agree insurance is very important, and if you have a policy to go over with him, well. . . I'm sorry but you'll just have to wait until he's back in the office tomorrow."

Jack saw the corners of Bernice's eyes tear up when she finished speaking. She reached over to her right and pulled a tissue out of a Kleenex box that sat on the upper corner of her desk. She dabbed at the corners of her eyes, drying them with the tissue.

"Did I say something to offend you, ma'am?" Jack asked. "I'm sorry if I was out of line or spoke inappropriately a moment ago. I know I may have come across as flippant about the boy's death, and I am sorry to hear such news. It's just that I. . . I strongly believe in what I do. Life insurance isn't just about us making money, you see. It's really about providing for those you love and leave behind after you've gone. To make sure they're provided for and don't go on struggling financially. It's hard enough on the emotions. It doesn't need to be so hard on the purse strings."

You're such a dog, Jack, he thought. *If you weren't so good at what you really do, you could do this. Hell, selling's right up your alley. You could sell ice to an Eskimo in the middle of the winter.*

"Mr. Pittman, you didn't offend me," Bernice replied. "Not at all. I'm just a little emotional right now. You see, it was just a couple of months ago that Ernie—my husband—died. He never got any insurance on himself. Said it was 'nothin' but a rip-off by them big companies,' and then he went and died and left me with so little. I've got my job here and all that, but it barely pays the bills. Half the time I have to ask Father Brennan for some help. And bless his heart, he does help. I get most of my groceries through here, but there are some things I can't buy that I need. Like my blood pressure medicine. And then Father Brennan's former housekeeper's son gets killed, and I don't remember Father Brennan saying if that family had a policy on the boy or not. Life's just so hard, you know. . . I'm sorry, here I am going on like this, telling you all my troubles, when that poor woman has enough of her own. What with her boy getting shot down like he did."

"I'm sorry to hear that, Mrs. Abernathy," Jack replied. "I thought I heard you tell that lady on the phone—Mrs. Sanders, was it?—that you didn't have any of the details."

Bernice winked again at Jack, then said, "Well, it was just a little white lie I told her, that's all. That Mrs. Sanders is such a busybody. Probably the city's biggest gossip. I figured it was best for everybody that she didn't know much about what happened last night to the boy. Keep her from spreading it all over this side of the city. Making that boy's poor mother even more upset when everybody would hear about it. Before she even has a chance to properly grieve for him."

"You know Mrs. Sanders is just going to go and dig the details out of Father Brennan when she meets with him tomorrow," Jack said. Then he added, "I can't say I blame you. Really I can't. I'd probably do the exact same thing. Some of my clients are just like her. They buy their policies, and pay their premiums to my company on time and all, and they think that entitles them to go and ask me what kinds of policies their neighbors bought. And how much their coverages are. Nosing into somebody else's business. I guess maybe to keep up with the Joneses and all that. Of course, bound by my professional ethics, I can't tell them anything. But they sure do ask."

"I'm sure they do. And I'm glad to hear you guard your clients' privacy so well."

"That I do, Mrs. Abernathy, that I do," Jack replied. He realized he needed to change the direction of this conversation rather quickly. As good as he thought he could be as a salesman it wasn't what he was here for. He needed to find Father Brennan for the real business he had with him. "I'd appreciate it if you could be so kind as to tell me, Mrs. Abernathy, where I can find his housekeeper so I can then find him. So I can deliver this policy to him. He has to sign it. You see, I have to return to Baton Rouge tomorrow and I'd like to wrap this up today. He's the last of my clients I have to see on this trip over here. I'm sure he'd understand my sense of urgency."

"Mr. Pittman, I really can't do that. Like you, I have *my* job to do, and I'm not at liberty to tell you where he is right now."

Jack noted the change in her voice again and the almost defensive posture she was now taking. He figured she was just protecting the priest, out of loyalty to him.

"This really isn't a good time anyway, with what happened," she continued. "I'm sure you'd agree. Besides, I don't know where she lives, and even if I did, Father Brennan wouldn't want me to go and tell you where he is."

"You sure are making it difficult for me, ma'am," Jack stated. "I just want to get this policy to him, review it with him, answer any questions he may have, and get him to sign it. I'll simply leave him his copy after all that's done and then I'll be on my way. I promise I'm not as insensitive as you think, with what's occurred. But I do have my job to do and I won't be back in New Orleans for another month or so."

Bernice leaned forward in her chair and said, quite emphatically, "I told you I can't tell you." The tone in her voice changed even more, as did her demeanor. "Now, Mr. Pittman, of the Northern Gulf Coast Life Insurance Company, is there anything else I can do for you today? Because if there isn't, I have a phone call I need to return. To one of *my* clients."

"No, ma'am, I guess there isn't anything else," Jack replied. "I suppose I'll have to call the archdiocese office and tell them Father Brennan's policy can't be put in force because he hasn't signed it." He was trying one last time to play on her emotions, to make her feel guilty for being so reluctant to help him.

"What, for him to die without a life insurance policy, Mr. Pittman?" Bernice said. "Don't you know Catholic priests take vows of poverty? Money doesn't mean anything to them, Mr. Pittman. They do what they do because of God's calling in their lives. And God surely called *that* man. I've never seen anyone like him. He loves to serve others, and it pains him to know someone might die and not make it to heaven because they didn't know the Father or His Son. That, Mr. Pittman, is what Father Brennan is all about. No life insurance policy is going to make that big a difference to him." She paused, then added, "I always thought the Church would take care of him anyway. It's really none of my business, but I don't see why he bought a policy in the first place."

Bernice had folded her arms across her chest and was glaring hard at Jack. He had the distinct impression that she saw right through him. That he was a charlatan or some kind of con artist. Maybe she was thinking something like, *Lecture's over. Now beat it, mister.* He figured it was best to drop it and move on. He'd have to find another way to locate the priest. He remembered the warning in the intel report, but he'd have to ignore it and go to the church anyway. Maybe he'd get lucky and find someone there who was a little more cooperative. And a little less protective of the priest.

"I'm sorry to have bothered you, Mrs. Abernathy," Jack replied. "I'll just have my office call him and set an appointment for some time next month. Good day to you, ma'am." He picked up his briefcase, turned, and walked out the door into the bright sunlight. He set his mind on the task ahead, determined to find out where Father Brennan's former housekeeper lives.

Find her, Jack, and you find the priest, he thought. *Put an end to this and then go have a nice meal.*

CHAPTER 7

Jack made his way from the Catholic Charities Office, first southward down Howard Avenue, then briefly onto the roundabout at Lee Circle. He followed its curve to the right until it released him back onto St. Charles.

He was headed west again, and drove quickly out of the Warehouse/Arts District. It was stop and go now, but finally the traffic signals changed and allowed him to pass under the wide, elevated U.S. Highway 90, known to locals as the Pontchartrain Expressway. When he was clear of the overpass he entered into the blissful surroundings of the Garden District. He found himself accompanied by a steady procession of the tourist-laden green-colored St. Charles streetcars as he drove past the manicured lawns and the stately houses that stood guard along the tree-lined avenue, preserving and protecting their long-held secrets of the western side of the sprawling city. He drove past the few businesses and an occasional church or school that served to break the steady westward march of those houses.

After passing the campus of Loyola University on his right and the huge city park and zoo on his left, he saw the spires of the Sacred Heart of Jesus Catholic Church rising upward toward the cloudless blue sky. Nearing the church Jack couldn't help but notice its impressive gothic architectural style and the well-manicured lawn and shrubbery surrounding the building. *Lots of money being poured into this one*, he thought. He pulled into the east-side parking lot, found an empty space there, pulled into it, and shut off the engine to the Cutlass. He reached over to his right, picked up the briefcase that was lying on the front passenger seat, and got out of the car. He pressed the LOCK button on the driver-side door, closed it, and walked toward the front of the church.

Jack hurried up the concrete steps leading to the front entrance to the church and entered the cool, dimly lit sanctuary. He noticed the small, stainless-steel bowls mounted on the walls at the entrance to the church. Subconsciously—like a golfer whose muscle memory automatically takes over when swinging a club for the first time in years—he reached out with his right hand and dipped his fingertips into the water in one of the bowls. He placed his fingertips to his forehead, then on his chest. He continued with his hand to his left shoulder and ended on his right. *The sign of the cross*, he reminded himself. *I haven't done that in years. I guess some things you never forget how to do.*

He entered the sanctuary and glanced toward the front of the church; he spotted an elderly black man at work on one of the kneelers at the foot of the altar. As he walked forward other memories of his own childhood church came back vividly. In his mind's eye he saw himself going forward, at the proper time in the service, to kneel on the hard wooden steps of the altar, waiting for the priest to come; Jack remembered watching and waiting breathlessly for Father De Marco to step in front of him and reach into the gold chalice and gently extract a small, round wafer from it. He remembered extending his tongue to receive that wafer, which he was taught to believe was the actual body of Christ; rising from the kneeler, he made his way slowly, quietly, reverently back to his seat to reflect on what sacrifices the Son of God made on his behalf. *Stop it, Jack, stop it*, he thought. *Quit thinking of all that. Remember why you're here.*

"Excuse me, sir," Jack called out to the worker. "Could you direct me to the church office? I'm looking for Father Edward Brennan. I was told he might be here this afternoon."

The old man looked at the younger man standing in front of him, sizing him up. He glanced at the coat, the tie, the nice haircut, and the briefcase he was holding so tightly in his left hand. He'd seen so many of his kind before.

"Young man, if you're here to sell somethin' to Father Brennan, then you're here at the wrong time. First of all, he ain't here right now. Second, he ain't got no money to buy whatever you sellin'. But you look like you 'bout to try anyway." The old man turned away from Jack, back toward his work. With his left hand, he motioned to an open doorway directly opposite where he stood. "You can go on if you want. The office is through that side door. Down the hall, first door on the right."

"Thank you," Jack said as he turned toward the open doorway. After a couple of steps, he stopped and turned back to the old man. "Not that it matters, but I'm not a salesman. I'm here to deliver some important legal papers to Father Brennan on behalf of my law firm."

He didn't know why he felt the need to say that; after all, it was a lie. Just another in a series of lies. Jack was good at them—very, very good at dishing them out. The trick was in keeping them straight, in not getting them mixed up like some amateur would. Doing so would trip him up, and so he worked hard at staying one step ahead of them. Later, if the police got involved, there would be so many confusing, contradictory stories told by witnesses to the investigators that it would take months to unravel what they were being told. Jack wondered how many cases went cold on his behalf. Did they just throw up their hands in disgust and frustration as a result of his skill at stretching the truth over the years?

***

Jack entered the church office and found a twenty-something black woman sitting at the receptionist's desk. She looked much younger than Bernice back at the Catholic Charities Office. By about twenty years. *Maybe this one will be more helpful,* he thought. He would try a different approach.

She looked up and saw Jack and said, "Good afternoon, sir. How may I help you today?"

"Good afternoon, ma'am. My name is Richard Pittman," Jack said. "I represent the law firm of Jacobs, Anderson, McNaulty, and Braswell of Houston, Texas. I'm here to see Father Edward Brennan. I understand he is the associate parish priest here. Is that correct?"

"That's right," the receptionist answered. "However, he's not in today. Is there something I can help you with?"

Jack saw the nameplate on her desk. Shalanda Jackson. "Ms. Jackson, my firm represents the interest of his family, most notably his mother, and I have some very important legal documents to review with him," Jack lied. "I was hoping to find him here this afternoon."

"His family, you said? His mother—is she all right?" Shalanda asked.

"Everyone's fine. No need to be alarmed."

"That's good. I was afraid his mother got sick again. Last time she did, Father Brennan flew all the way up to St. Louis. Found her in the hospital. Later on he told me she'd been there *three days* before anyone called him to come see her. He was real upset about that. Anyway, I'm glad she's okay. You had me worried there for a minute."

"Yes, well, I do apologize for that misunderstanding," Jack said. "At any rate, I do need to see him so I can show him the papers I have with me. It's very important that I meet with him soon." He paused, then said, "My job won't be finished unless I do that." This time he wasn't lying.

"Well, Mr. Pittman," Shalanda began, "as I said, Father Brennan's not here today. He should be back tomorrow morning. When I see him, I'll be glad to tell him you came by." She waited a moment; sensing this wasn't what the man in front of her wanted to hear, she asked, "If you want, I can make an appointment for you in the morning." She glanced down at the appointment book on her desk. "How about 9:30?" she said when she looked up again.

"Normally that would be fine, but I'm booked on a flight back to Houston much earlier than that. If you could tell me where he is, I'll just go see him and get these legal documents reviewed and signed. Then I'll be on my way."

"I'm not able to do that, Mr. Pittman," she said. "He's not on official church business. That means I'm not able to tell you where he is."

"If you can't tell me, Ms. Jackson, could you get someone who can?" Jack replied. "Your supervisor, perhaps? Is he in today?"

"*She* is in, sir. Hold on. I'll get Sister Margaret for you."

Jack watched as Shalanda got up from her chair, turned, and entered an office behind her desk. Jack heard a muffled conversation between her and another female in the office. He assumed it was Sister Margaret, whom she had mentioned. A few minutes later a petite, rather pretty young woman appeared through the opened doorway of that office. She was dressed in a black knee-length skirt and a white blouse that was buttoned tightly around her neck. A small silver cross dangled from a thin chain hanging around her neck. She wore no other jewelry—no earrings dangled from her ears, and she wore no rings on any of her fingers. Her thin, light-brown hair was cut shoulder length and complemented her hazel eyes. Jack noticed she wore no makeup, but he noticed, too, there was no need for her to do so. *A natural beauty*, he thought. *And a nun! They didn't make them that pretty when I was a kid.*

He recalled the images of Sister Angela and Sister Catherine from St. Michael's School back in Pensacola. Sister Angela was rugged looking, built like a linebacker. Sister Catherine was as tall and rail-thin as Timmy Murphy, the center on the school's eighth-grade basketball team. *No broken hearts when those two hit the convent*, Jack remembered joking to his seventh-grade friends.

He was certain that was not the case with this nun. *Sister, you must have caused a few young men to cry themselves to sleep when you went in*, he thought.

"Good morning," she said to Jack. "My name is Sister Margaret," she added as she extended her hand.

"Pleased to meet you, Sister Margaret," Jack said. "My name is Richard Pittman and—"

"Shalanda told me your name," Sister Margaret interrupted, "and she also told me you have come from Houston to speak with Father Brennan about some legal business to attend to with him. She also told me she mentioned to you that Father Brennan is not here this afternoon, and yet you still needed to speak with me. Am I correct, Mr. Pittman?"

"That is correct, Sister Margaret," Jack replied, wondering why she was so curt with him. He withdrew a business card from his right outer coat pocket. One from another set printed by Eddie Trask. He extended the card to Sister Margaret. She took the card and inspected it carefully.

"Sister Margaret, as I told Ms. Jackson—Shalanda—I represent the law firm of Jacobs, Anderson, McNaulty, and Braswell of Houston, Texas. It's imperative that I meet with Father Brennan today."

Sister Margaret looked up from the business card she was clutching and affixed her gaze on Jack. Jack returned the look, again noticing the hazel-colored eyes. He found himself staring at her. He was embarrassed by it, but he couldn't stop looking at her. *God, you're so pretty*, he thought. And then it dawned on him how he was *supposed* to act and feel. *Stop it, Jack. She's a nun, for God's sake.*

"Well, Mr. Pittman. You may have some legal matters to discuss with Father Brennan, but you *won't* be able to do that today. He's not returning to the office until tomorrow morning. Shalanda said she offered to schedule an appointment for the morning, but it appears you have other ideas, which seem to me to include my telling you where he is so you can see him anyway? Would that be correct, as well, Mr. Pittman?"

Man, she is a tough little thing, Jack thought. *Feisty, as well as pretty. Careful, Jack. You're walking on thin ice here. One misstep and you'll fall through.* "Look, Sister Margaret. I'm not trying to do anything underhanded," he replied aloud, lying again. "Or to get you or Ms. Jackson into any trouble. I just need to conclude my business with Father Brennan and then I'll be on my way." He wasn't lying when he said that. "I flew all the way in from Houston so I could meet with Father Brennan, and get him to review and sign the papers I have with me. Then he and his family can sell the property in question and they'll have enough money to take care of Mrs. Brennan up there in St. Louis. He's the last member of the immediate family that I have to see for his signature and agreement."

Jack was on a roll now. The lies were rolling off his tongue. He was hoping to seal the deal soon with Sister Margaret. Get her to come around to his way of thinking. She appeared to be listening quite carefully to what he had to say; the expression on her face told him she was, in fact, at least interested in what he was saying. The question posed itself in Jack's mind, *Yeah, but does she believe me?*

Sister Margaret nearly floored him when she spoke again. "Why didn't you say so sooner, Mr. Pittman?" she asked. "I'm aware of the situation with Father Brennan's mother in St. Louis. It's touch and go, to say the least. He told me just a few days ago that her health has not improved as dramatically as he had hoped. He said the family needed to come up with a substantial amount of money required for her proper care. I'm very concerned about this matter myself." She paused briefly before adding, "I suppose the sale of this property you speak of may be a solution to his dilemma. I'd like to do what I can to help. I hate to see Father Brennan so discouraged. It's so unlike him."

"Well, Sister Margaret, I don't know the man very well, but I do know if it were my own mother's health that was at risk and I could get my hands on the money needed for her care, I would certainly do so. Perhaps now you understand the rather urgent nature of my business with him. The sooner I find him the sooner the property can be sold and the money from the sale of said property can be made available to her up in St. Louis."

"Said property," Jack recalled saying. *Boy, you* are *good. You're beginning to sound just like a lawyer.*

"In that case, Mr. Pittman, I will tell you where to find him," Sister Margaret replied. "But you must promise to use discretion in your dealing with him when you do locate him. You see, his former housekeeper's son was killed last night in a drive-by shooting, a block from her apartment unit in the Desire Projects. Father Brennan is with her and her family right now. He was very close to the boy and the family when he served at St. John's out there on Louisa Street. He nearly fainted when he took the call from her and heard what had happened. He told me right away about it. Then he left immediately. So, Mr. Pittman, do you see why I am asking you to be brief and leave him once you have concluded your business with him? Please, let him comfort the family without too much interference. You *will* do that, won't you?"

"Oh yes, Sister, I most certainly will," Jack replied. "I *will definitely* leave once I have concluded my business with Father Brennan. You can count on it."

***

Jack walked back to the Cutlass, unlocked it, got in, and sat down. He placed the briefcase on the passenger seat and reached over to the glove compartment and opened it. He pulled out a City of New Orleans map he had placed there, unfolded it, and looked again at the address on the piece of paper Sister Margaret had given him. He found the Street Index on the lower left corner of the map and ran down the list of names until he found the one he was looking for. He pulled out a pen from his coat pocket and circled Abundance Avenue, and familiarized himself with the general area surrounding the street. It was well to the northeast of his present location. Out by the canal and the Intracoastal Waterway, south of the Lakefront Airport. He studied the map carefully, noting that he could take St. Charles back to the Pontchartrain Expressway, get on it, and take it north until it merged with I-10 near the Superdome. From there it looked like he had to take the interstate toward the east and get off at the Franklin Street exit. *A couple of zigs and a few zags later I should be there*, Jack thought. *Where I find the housekeeper, I find the priest.*

He folded the map to show the area around the Desire Projects and placed it on top of the briefcase next to him. He started the engine and was shifting into drive when he remembered what Shalanda had said to him as he was leaving the church office.

"Be careful, Mr. Pittman," she said. "A white man going into the 'Dirty D' needs to be *extra* careful. Don't go getting yourself killed in there."

CHAPTER 8

Traffic was heavy along St. Charles and it took Jack nearly thirty minutes to make the drive from the church to the Pontchartrain Expressway. He waited for the light above him to change, crossed under the southbound bridge, signaled, and made a left turn onto the northbound ramp. He accelerated quickly up the ramp and the Cutlass soon merged with the flow of traffic on the crowded highway. Within a few minutes, he spotted the Superdome on his right and a moment later he was merging with the flow of traffic headed east on I-10.

The sight of the Superdome jogged his memory—he still needed to purchase his Saints season tickets. Since he landed back in Pensacola a couple of years ago, he made it a point to get them in the spring for each upcoming season. *Here it is, almost the end of April, and I haven't gotten around to it,* he thought. Despite their poor win-loss records each year, Jack enjoyed watching the Saints play, especially when those despicable Falcons came to town. He loved being in the Superdome on a Sunday afternoon, cheering for Archie and the rest of the team. Like other Saints fans, he was hoping the upcoming season would be at least as good as it was two years ago, when they went 8 and 8. *Nothing could be as bad as last year's 1 and 15 record,* Jack thought. *Anything would be an improvement on that.*

He remembered reading a recent article in the sports section of the *Pensacola News Journal* that predicted with Bum Phillips as the new head coach and George Rogers, last year's Heisman Trophy winner from South Carolina, on the roster things were looking up for the Saints for the 1981 season. *Let's hope so,* Jack thought. *I don't want to join those Aints fans and go into the Dome with a paper bag over my head.*

He glanced to his right and saw the old St. Louis Cemetery below him, and he made a mental note to visit there again. It had been a while since he walked through the cemetery, looking at the crypts and tombs that sat above ground there, trying in vain to find the names of Jacques and Yvette Devereaux. He remembered his mother telling him her great-grandfather and great-grandmother were buried there, along with several of her other ancestors. He couldn't find the tomb the last time he was in town and he thought he'd try again tomorrow. *After I leave the Superdome box office with my Saints tickets. First things first.*

Seeing the cemetery below him brought back other memories. After he and his brothers were released from St. Michael's Catholic School for the summer, his parents would load up their black Ford station wagon, somehow squeezing themselves and their four boys and all their luggage in the car, for their annual trip to New Orleans each June.

His father, Frank Brantley, had been stationed at NAS New Orleans during World War II and had met and married Edith Devereaux when the war ended. He had taken her away from New Orleans back to his own hometown of Pensacola and that little house on W Street in Brownsville. She had cried when they left New Orleans, but he promised his new bride he would take a week of vacation each summer and they would go back so she could see her brother, sister, and old friends and relive her memories of growing up in the city.

Jack remembered they would stay at the home she grew up in; her brother Barry, being the eldest, had inherited the family home and he lived there with his wife Ellen. They didn't have children but they had that huge house in Old Metairie and didn't seem to mind having six additional people in their home for a few days. From there they would make the short drive each day to Gentilly, to see his mom's younger sister Colette.

Aunt Colette and her husband Dennis lived with their six children in a cramped four-bedroom, two-bath house in one of the older neighborhoods off Paris Avenue. Jack often thought how ironic it was that she missed out on inheriting the larger house; if she had, she and Uncle Dennis would have had much more room to house their large brood.

He remembered when they were at Aunt Colette's house in Gentilly, he and his three brothers would be forced to spend the morning and afternoon in the backyard with their six cousins while the grown-ups got to stay inside and enjoy the cooling effects of the recently installed central air-conditioning unit. The cousins would pout, saying, "It's not fair. It's so hot out here!" Jack and his brothers listened to it as long as they could, which was about thirty minutes. Being the eldest—as well as the most brazen and impatient—child in his family, Jack would turn to his cousins and tell them, "Grow up and quit whining. My brothers and I play outside in the summer all the time. You get used to it."

He thought of those trips fondly, remembering how exciting it was when they would all pile into their automobiles and head over to the amusement park at Pontchartrain Beach. There he and his brothers and their cousins would escape the heat of the day by changing at the bathhouse and plunging into one of the park's swimming pools. Later, when the sun would sink in the western sky and the air would cool down a little, the parents of the two families would head over to one of the park's concession stands and fill their kids up on their choice of hamburgers or hot dogs, fries or onion rings, and Cokes or a milkshake for dinner and then they would let the kids ride the roller coaster, the Ferris wheel, the carousel, and the other rides in the park.

A delivery truck cut in front of him unexpectedly and brought him out of his past. He saw that he was nearing the juncture with I-610 and he began looking for the Franklin Street exit. A minute or two more passed and then he spotted the sign for it. He moved over to the far-right lane and got on the exit ramp. He followed its long, sweeping curve until it ended and dumped him southbound onto Franklin. Traffic was heavy along the street and Jack drove in the bumper-to-bumper congestion looking for the crossroad of Florida Avenue. He saw it up ahead, and signaled to turn left. He waited for the oncoming traffic to clear, turned onto Florida, and went through the light at Almonaster. He ran parallel to the railroad tracks on his right and came to the intersection at Louisa. And another traffic light. He made a left turn quickly and found he was headed north, back toward the interstate. He wished there had been a closer exit than Franklin to have gotten him here, and wondered why it was planned that way.

The street map indicated there was an entrance into the projects somewhere up ahead and on his right. He drove a couple of blocks and then spotted the large sign for the Desire Housing Project. He turned right onto Abundance Avenue and immediately thought he had entered another world.

As he drove slowly along the street, Jack reached under his blazer, removed the .45 automatic from the holster, and laid it on the seat next to him. He was looking at the dilapidated, two-story brick-and-veneer buildings, searching for unit and apartment numbers, when a basketball suddenly shot out in front of him from the left. He turned his head to see where it came from and noticed a shirtless black boy darting in front of the Cutlass, running after the loose ball. Jack hit his brakes hard to avoid striking the boy. The boy looked like he was about fourteen, maybe fifteen, and his black skin glistened with sweat. He had not bothered to look at Jack's Cutlass; he just kept running after the ball, which was now rolling across the blacktop toward the curb on the other side. Jack looked again to his left; three other boys were standing on the half-court. One was shirtless and sweating profusely, while the other two were clad in sweat-stained, short-sleeved white T-shirts. They were yelling at the first boy, urging him to retrieve the ball and return to continue their pick-up game.

Two on two. Shirts versus skins, Jack thought. It was all too familiar to him. The same way he and his brothers had played *their* games on the small court at the public elementary school close to their house in Pensacola. They played rough, hard games that lasted all afternoon under a hot sun, and sweated profusely, just like these boys. He had always played shirtless, proud of his tan, muscled upper body.

After picking up the loose ball and cradling it under his left arm, Shirtless Boy turned and walked slowly as he crossed the street in front of Jack's car. Jack watched as the boy flashed a toothy grin and made a thumbs-up gesture, signaling to his buddies he was about to mess with the white man in the shiny silver car. Cradling the basketball under his left arm, Shirtless Boy walked over to the driver-side window of the Cutlass and rapped on the glass with his knuckles. Jack rolled down the window.

"Dang, mister," the boy said, staring at the white man inside. "You know you almost kill me? Nearly scare me to death. Like to give me a heart attack." He flashed his toothy grin at Jack. "What my momma say if you went an' run me over and send me to the hospital?"

"I don't know," Jack replied, "and I really don't care. If she was smart, she might thank me, just to get you out of her hair for a few days." Jack wasn't smiling.

"Oh, man. Why you got to go and say somethin' like that?" the boy said. He looked at Jack with defiance. Jack knew the look. "My friends ain't gonna like you talkin' to me like that." He held up his hand and motioned for the others to come over. Jack glanced their way and saw they had started walking toward his car.

Jack returned his gaze and stared hard at Shirtless Boy. "That isn't the only thing they won't like," he said as he raised the .45 and leveled it at Shirtless Boy's face. "Now beat it, you little punk."

Shirtless Boy's mouth dropped open as he stared into the barrel of the gun in his face. Jack smiled as the kid suddenly turned and ran toward the basketball court and his waiting friends. They noticed the gun in Jack's hand and stopped walking, wanting no part of this encounter. Jack watched a moment longer to ensure the kid was indeed back with his friends and was well out of his way. Then he let off the brake and continued driving down Abundance Avenue.

He was looking for the address on the piece of paper Sister Margaret had given him and was interested in far bigger prey than those four kids.

***

Jack spotted Building E on his left and pulled into a parking lot directly across from it. He left the engine running and turned the air-conditioner setting to low and the fan switch on high. Soon it was nice and cool inside the Cutlass, and from where he sat he could see the front door of Apartment 232. It was a downstairs unit, uncluttered and clean-looking. Unlike the ones next to it. Several well-tended potted plants sat on the stoop to the left and right of the door. No grass grew in the dirt in front of the apartment, nor in front of the rest of the building; its dark soil had been swept clean, however. Jack looked to the left of the unit, at Building D, then to the right, at Building F, and noticed the grassless soil in front of those buildings was littered with empty soda and beer cans, cigarette butts, and wind-blown papers and candy wrappers. He looked back at the housekeeper's building and noticed all the stoops and door fronts both upstairs and down had been recently repainted and their own potted plants were well-tended. The adjacent buildings looked old and decrepit with their sagging, weather-beaten fronts. It appeared to him Father Brennan's former housekeeper and the others in her building worked hard at making this hellish place a little more tolerable.

All he could do now was sit and watch and wait for signs of life coming from Apartment 232. He didn't want to be here any longer than he had to; he was looking forward to the Shrimp Amandine at Galatoire's tonight.

***

Jack glanced down at his watch. Twenty minutes had passed and there was still no sign of the former housekeeper or her family, let alone the priest. Maybe he had the wrong address and was looking at the wrong building. He reread the information on the slip of paper Sister Margaret had handed him. *The Desire Projects. Abundance Avenue, Building E, Apartment 232.* Assuming she had provided him with the correct address, he formed two conclusions: A, they weren't at home right now, or B, they were in there but weren't ready to come out anytime soon. *Only one way to find out*, he thought.

He shut off the engine, put the .45 back in the holster beneath his blazer, grabbed the briefcase from the passenger seat, and opened the door to the Cutlass. He stepped out into the glare of the bright sun and immediately felt the heavy, humid air envelop him. He loosened his tie, gripped the handle of the briefcase, pressed the LOCK button, and closed the door to the Cutlass and walked across the hot parking lot.

***

Jack stepped off the asphalt onto the grassless soil surrounding Building E. As he walked toward Apartment 232 the image of Attucks Court on Cervantes Street in Pensacola flashed in his mind. It had been built by the Pensacola Area Housing Commission as a single-level, low-income housing unit, and each time Jack entered it he felt the despair and hopelessness his friend Marcus Robinson must have felt. He wondered if the same despair was felt by the residents here.

He began to think back to the time, thirteen years ago, when he had become friends with Marcus at the beginning of the summer entering their senior year. Scrimmages had been held at Pensacola's Catholic high school, pitting the area's best athletes—black and white—against one another; the county school superintendent wanted the point made to everyone concerned that the federally mandated integration order for the upcoming fall was here to stay. The economy of the city and county was heavily dependent upon the United States Naval Air Station, and the constant ebb and flow of the many educated and progressive-minded pilots and their families persuaded the school board to concede to the forced integration of its schools with little fanfare. Some instances of racial animosity popped up from time to time after that, but for the most part any ill will between blacks and whites was put aside that fall. *Money, and King Football, had a way of doing that*, Jack thought when he looked back upon it all a few years later.

September's games came and went, and with the cooler weather of October came *the Game* between the city's rival schools. While Jack played defense and was the starting free safety for the Tigers of Pensacola High, Marcus was the first-string fullback for Washington High's high-octane offense. The Tigers entered the contest confident victory was theirs for the taking, but Marcus and his Wildcats teammates thrashed Jack and the Tigers before a packed house at Tiger Stadium. The next day Jack's body still ached from the numerous blows he received from Marcus each time he broke into the Tigers' secondary and ran over and through Jack on his way to scoring his five touchdowns that evening.

Jack and Marcus had become good friends, as close as the society of that deep-South city would allow a white and a black to get, and he came to the Court looking for his friend. Jack remembered how cool and windy the weather was that mid-October Saturday afternoon as he walked up to Marcus's apartment. He also remembered the shock and anguish when Marcus's mother came to the door and told him that her son had been killed earlier in the morning by an angry teammate who had accused Marcus of running off with his girlfriend after the game.

Jack knocked on the door of 232 Abundance Avenue and was wondering why the housekeeper's son had been gunned down when the door to the apartment opened. A young black girl of about fourteen, maybe fifteen, years of age stood in the doorway. She appeared to have been crying for quite some time. Jack noticed she was wearing a white blouse and a navy-blue-and-green plaid skirt. He glanced at the patch that was sewn onto the left pocket of her blouse. *St. John's Catholic High School*. She must be the daughter of Father Brennan's former housekeeper, the same housekeeper Sister Margaret told him about while he was at the church office at Sacred Heart.

"May I help you?" she asked. She dabbed at her eyes with a very damp, very wadded-up tissue she held in her right hand.

"Good afternoon, miss. I was wondering if I may speak with your father or mother," Jack replied.

"My daddy's not here right now, but my mama is. May I tell her what this is about?" She dabbed the tissue at the corners of her eyes.

Jack pulled a business card from the lower left pocket of his jacket and handed it to the girl at the door. It was from another set Eddie had prepared and given him. "Would you let her know that I represent the Tri-State Insurance Company out of Jackson, Mississippi? I'd like to discuss how my company may be of service to her. And her husband, of course."

"This may not be a good time, Mr.. . ." the girl replied.

"Patterson. Raymond Patterson," Jack said, pointing to the card in the young girl's hand.

". . .Mr. Patterson," the girl said as she looked at the card. "My older brother was killed last night and my daddy is at the funeral home, and mama is with Father Brennan in the kitchen. She's been crying an awful long time."

A male voice suddenly called out from somewhere in the apartment. "Cassandra, who's at the door?"

Cassandra turned to reply. "Some man saying he'd like to speak to my mama, Father. He said he's from some insurance company."

"The Tri-State Insurance Company," Jack reminded her.

Jack saw a middle-aged, slightly balding white man come to the door, dressed in the all too familiar black business attire of a Catholic priest. He spoke quietly to the young girl.

"Thank you, Cassandra," he said as he took the card from her hand. "Why don't you go into the kitchen with your mother while I speak to this young man?"

Cassandra walked away from the priest toward the back of the apartment. The priest examined the card and read it aloud.

"Raymond Patterson. Sales Agent. Life, Health, and Annuities. The Tri-State Insurance Company. Jackson, Mississippi." The priest looked up from the card he held in his right hand. "How may I help you, Mr. Patterson?"

"Well, sir. . ." Jack started to say. "I'm sorry, I should address you as Father, shouldn't I? Are you Catholic or Episcopalian?"

"Catholic," the priest replied. "Unlike you I don't have a card on me, but allow me to introduce myself. I'm Father Edward Brennan, of the Archdiocese of New Orleans," he added. "The Sacred Heart of Jesus Catholic Church on St. Charles Avenue. Tell me, Mr. Patterson, what brings you to this neighborhood?"

"Yes, well, Father Brennan, my company is doing a survey in this area, trying to ascertain the insurance needs of its residents. But it would appear I have called upon this apartment at a very unfortunate time. The young lady—Cassandra, I believe that's her name—informed me her brother had been killed last night. I am so sorry to hear that. I don't mean to be callous at such a time as this." He paused for effect. "I only hope the family had insurance to cover his final expenses."

"Young man, you have indeed come at a very inconvenient time. I know you have a job to do, and you must make a living. But a tragedy has struck this home and I must ask you to please leave. Now, if I may, I need to get back to them," Father Brennan said as he stepped back from the door and began to close it.

"I will, Father. I will leave. And you will accompany me," Jack said as he pulled the .45 automatic from the holster and leveled it at the priest's chest. "Now, I'll ask you to be very calm and quiet in doing so." He paused, motioning to the interior of the apartment, and said, "Just tell the girl and her mother that you have an urgent business matter to attend to back at the church and you must leave unexpectedly. *Please*. Father."

The priest looked down at the gun pointed at him, then looked back up incredulously at Jack. "There must be some mistake, young man," he calmly stated. "Can't you see I am a priest? What do you want with *me*? Get that thing out of my sight!"

"I can't do that, Father," Jack replied. "Now, as I said before, please inform them of your need to leave and let them know you will talk to them later. Do it now, Father. Do not underestimate me or force me to do something that will be very unpleasant for you. Or them."

"You really aren't 'Raymond Patterson,' are you?" Father Brennan asked.

"Just do as I say." Jack stepped closer to the priest. "Or do you want me to involve them in this matter between the two of us?"

"No, son, there is no need for that," Father Brennan replied. He turned toward the interior of the apartment. "Cassandra, would you please come into the living room?" he asked.

Cassandra appeared in the doorway between the kitchen and the living room. "Yes, Father?"

"Cassandra, would you tell your mother I have some rather urgent business to attend to back at Sacred Heart? Please tell her I may not return until. . ." Father Brennan turned to face Jack. "Until. . .?" he asked Jack.

"Just tell her you'll get back with them as soon as you can," Jack whispered, glaring at the priest. "Don't make this any harder than it needs to be, Father."

"Cassandra, tell your mother I will talk to her tomorrow," Father Brennan continued.

"Okay, Father," she said as she turned and disappeared into the kitchen.

The priest turned back to face Jack. "Now, young man, I don't know what your business is with me, and I will do as you ask. Not for my sake, but for theirs. There will be no need for anything, as you said, *unpleasant* to occur to them. I will go with you. Now, if you will be so kind as to step aside, you and I will be on our way," Father Brennan said as he closed the door to the apartment behind him.

The priest walked in front of Jack and stepped off the small porch of the apartment onto the grassless soil. Jack moved in behind him, holding the gun level at the small of the priest's back. He heard the door to the apartment open behind him and heard a female voice.

"Father Brennan," the voice cried out. "I know Fred is going to ask me if you agreed to say Mass at the funeral for Marcus. You will, won't you, Father?"

Father Brennan continued to walk in front of Jack. He turned his head slightly in the woman's direction and replied, "Of course, Estelle, of course I will." He then said to Jack, "Now, young man, I assume you have a vehicle somewhere in the vicinity. Where is it, and where are we really headed? I know it's not to my church."

Man, the kid's name was Marcus, also. Jack was lost in thought for a moment. "What?" he replied aloud. "Oh yeah, Father. Head toward that silver Cutlass in the parking lot across the street."

"Father, is everything okay?" Jack heard the woman yell as he and the priest continued toward the car.

"Just keep moving, Father," Jack stated.Father Brennan did as Jack ordered and continued to walk toward the parking lot.

Estelle and Cassandra stood on the front stoop of their apartment and watched the two men walk away from them.

"What did you say was the name of that young white man, Cassandra?" Estelle asked.

"He said his name is Raymond Patterson. Some kind of salesman," she replied. "Insurance, I think it was. Why do you ask, mama?"

"Well, child, don't it seem kinda strange to you here comes some white man into this place and off he goes with Father Brennan?" she asked. "Where is that card of his? Salesmen always got a card on them."

"He gave me one, and I gave it to Father Brennan when he asked for it," Cassandra said. "I guess Father Brennan still has it."

"Strange, that's all I can say, child," Estelle said. "Real strange."

They watched a while longer as Father Brennan and the young man stood at the left side of the vehicle. They saw the young man reach into his pocket, pull out a key, and unlock and open the driver side door of the silver car. They saw Father Brennan get in and sit down in the driver seat, and they watched the young man push the door shut; he walked around to the other side of the vehicle, got in, and pulled his door shut. They heard the engine start and watched as Father Brennan backed out of the parking space and pulled forward onto Abundance Avenue. The silver car turned left, rounded the slight curve in the road, and disappeared.

"Mama, that does seem strange," Cassandra said. "Father Brennan is driving that man's car, and leaving his over there in the parking lot. Why do you think that man had Father do that?"

"Yeah, Cassandra, it is strange," her mother replied. "But white folks sure enough do some strange things anyway." She turned toward the front door. "Even Father Brennan. I've known that man an awful long time and he do the strangest things sometimes. Why one time, it was Halloween a few years back, when he was still at St. John's and I was just finishin' makin' his dinner at the rectory, and he comes in dressed up like that Frankenstein monster. Sat down at the table. Acted like it was normal, somethin' he did every day. Then he looked at me again and started laughin', thinkin' it was real funny. Shoot, wasn't nothin' funny about that, far as I could see."

Estelle turned to go back inside the apartment.

"Well, child, let's get inside. Your daddy will be home soon and we got lots of things to do."

PART TWO

FOUND

CHAPTER 9

The alarm beeped and Jack rolled over toward the clock and noted the time: *7:00.* He hit the SNOOZE button and drifted back to sleep. It beeped again fifteen minutes later and he reached over, shut it off, and slowly pulled himself upright in the bed. He put a pillow behind his head and leaned back against the headboard. The fog in his brain was slowly beginning to lift as he reached over to the nightstand and pulled a cigarette out of the pack and lit it. He inhaled the smoke deep into his lungs, desperate for the first of the day's nicotine to course its way into his system. He tried not to think, but the harder he tried the more he thought anyway. He began recalling the visit by the demons; he wondered if their intrusions would ever end, and if the memories of Vietnam would ever go away. He wished to God they would someday.

He had dreamed of the little boy as if it were yesterday. He remembered seeing himself yelling at the six- or seven-year-old, ordering him to no avail to drop the grenade he held in his hand. He saw the boy pull the pin and cock his arm to throw it into the LT's tent; then he saw himself fire two rounds from his .45 into the kid's chest and watched as the kid fell backward, dead before he ever hit the ground. He watched as the grenade landed at the boy's side, blowing his small head and right arm and leg off his tiny body. He watched again as the boy's insides spilled out, watched as the blood pooled beside him, unable to penetrate the hard, sunbaked ground.

Brainwashing those little village kids, getting them to do stuff like that! he thought. *I hope you VC are rotting in hell!*

He wondered if God ever could, or would, forgive him for what he did. He knew he had to do it to save the LT, and he also knew he lost his soul that very day. Each time he awoke from this dream, he was certain of it. Besides, the demons were there to remind him, just in case he ever forgot.

He began to focus again, to get his mind away from it. He needed to simply think of the next thing to do, and maybe another minor function beyond that one. Finish the cigarette. Hit the head. Get some coffee. *One step at a time, Jack, one step at a time*, he thought. It was the only thing he could think to do.

He stumbled to the bathroom, flipped on the light, and stood at the toilet emptying his bladder for what seemed like an eternity. A slight temptation surfaced in his mind to head back to the bed for some more sleep, but he knew he could do no such thing—there were more urgent things calling out to him to be done today. Besides, the demons might return; they usually waited until the dark of night, but they could very well come in the day if he allowed them to. He wasn't about to begin. He couldn't take that chance.

He finished, flushed the toilet, and turned to the sink. Leaning against it, he stared at himself in the mirror. He felt exhausted; it was showing on his face. The dark circles under his eyes were beginning to concern him, and he wondered how much longer it would be before his mind and body gave in and he collapsed from the broken sleep. As much as he wanted to, he knew returning to bed would serve no purpose.

He turned the handle for the cold water, splashed some on his face, rubbed it into his eyes, dried off. He looked at himself in the mirror once again. Not much better than before. *What the heck*, he thought as he walked out of the bathroom and headed for the kitchen, and the coffee maker that beckoned. All he had to do was flip the on switch and the magic elixir would begin to drip into the pot. *I can handle that.*

He waited until he heard the first gurgle and hiss of the machine before he walked over and opened the refrigerator door. He stood in front of it, staring absentmindedly inside. Its contents held nothing of interest to him. He closed the door, walked back to the counter, and stood in front of the coffeepot, waiting for the coffee to finish dripping into the pot. Drip, drip, drip. An eternity, it seemed.

He was counting on the first cup to finally clear the fog; a second to begin thinking clearly. Anything after that was simply to get him wired for the day ahead.

***

Jack finished showering, shaving, and downing another cup of coffee before he ambled back down the hallway to the kitchen. The caffeine began working its way through his system; he was beginning to feel as though he *would* somehow make it through the morning. And making it through the morning would get him through the rest of the day. He finished towel drying his hair, and ran his fingers through it in a feeble attempt at combing it. He poured himself another cup and carried it with him into the living room.

He turned on the television and held the switch until he found Channel 5 out of Mobile. He stood in front of the set watching Mel Showers, the morning anchor for the station, wrap up a story about an accident between a tractor trailer rig and two cars just beyond the exit of the eastbound interstate tunnel earlier in the morning. It was still not cleared completely and Mel reported it would tie up traffic heading across the bay to the Eastern Shore area for at least another two hours. Jack breathed a sigh of relief, knowing he would be heading in the opposite direction through the westbound tunnel later this morning; the traffic snarl wouldn't interfere with what he had to do today in the city. He walked back into the kitchen, fixed a bowl of cereal, and walked over to the small dinette and sat down to watch the rest of the morning news show while he ate.

Mel Showers had turned the show over to the meteorologist, and Jack half listened to the man drone on about the high and low temperatures for the day, the noticeable lack of rain lately, and the forecast for the next several days. Then it was back to Mel, and the story he began telling immediately caught Jack's attention.

"For those of you in the Channel 5 viewing area who are just joining us, good Thursday morning to all of you," Mel stated. He continued. "We begin by recapping the story we reported during last night's broadcast. Police in New Orleans are requesting that anyone who may have information regarding the whereabouts of Father Edward Brennan of the Archdiocese of New Orleans to please contact them at the number at the bottom of your screen." In addition to the phone number, Jack saw the station was showing a recent photograph of the priest.

Mel continued reading. "As mentioned at the beginning of this hour, Father Brennan, the associate parish priest at the Sacred Heart of Jesus Catholic Church, located on St. Charles Avenue, was last seen in the company of a white male late Tuesday afternoon. They were reported by two residents of the Desire Housing Projects to have left in a late-model four-door silver sedan. Though the make, model, and license number of the vehicle are unknown at the present time, the residents—a mother and her teenage daughter—were able to provide police a detailed description of the man who accompanied Father Brennan. They described him as approximately thirty to thirty-five years of age, with light-brown, neatly trimmed hair, brown eyes, five feet nine or ten inches tall, weighing approximately one hundred seventy to one hundred seventy-five pounds. He was wearing a navy-blue blazer, tan slacks, white shirt, and striped tie. The New Orleans Police Department has not gone on record to say if foul play is involved as the residents reporting the incident said Father Brennan didn't appear to be threatened in any way. As of this broadcast, however, Father Brennan has not been seen at Sacred Heart Church, nor has he reported in at the Catholic Charities Office on Baronne Street, where he serves as the administrator there on weekday afternoons.

"Again, if you have any information regarding the disappearance of Father Edward Brennan, please contact the New Orleans Police Department at the number on your screen. All calls will remain confidential."

Jack turned off the television, got up, and walked over to the kitchen sink and placed the coffee mug and cereal bowl in it. He figured by now the Hertz rental agency at the airport would have reported the rented Cutlass as missing; certainly the New Orleans Police would have found it by now where he abandoned it on Poydras Street. Maybe they have, and they're not reporting it to the public yet. *Doesn't matter anyway*, he thought. *What's done is done.*

He knew the police would find it sooner or later; they'd dust it for prints but wouldn't find any. He left it clean, no prints. Nothing to tie it to him. He was careful and figured he was a step or two ahead of the police anyway. He was always cautious with them. *Sooner or later they're going to make some connections—the Catholic Charities Office on Baronne, the church on St. Charles, and the apartment on Abundance Avenue where the priest was last seen*, he thought. Hopefully it would end there for them. He was counting on it to be a dead end.

He knew there were uncertainties in his trade. Things happened that way. He was, however, a very cautious, calculating man, and tried his best to limit them. There were things he could only be hopeful for, and based on experience, he was counting on them to vigorously pursue the disappearance, exhaust all possible and probable leads, and then finally give up when they hit that dead end and realized that both Richard Pittman and Raymond Patterson did not exist and that Father Edward Brennan, who did, had simply vanished into thin air.

CHAPTER 10

Jack went back to the bedroom and packed some clothes into a duffel bag and placed the bag on the bed. He walked to the closet and pulled out three small boxes from the front left corner of the top shelf. He placed the boxes on the bed next to a second duffel bag and opened each box. He saw he had five loaded clips to his .45 in each of the first two; a third box contained two full boxes of 12-gauge buckshot. He reached into the corner of the closet and pulled out the sawed-off Remington Wingmaster he had placed there, and from his nightstand he pulled out the .45 ACP. He placed the weapons in the second duffel bag, along with the boxes of ammunition, and zipped it up.

He grabbed his prepacked travel shaving kit, picked up the other two bags, flipped off the light to the bedroom, and walked down the hall toward the living room. He placed the three bags next to the front door, then went into the kitchen. He filled a cooler with several cans of sodas and bottles of water and threw some ice from the freezer bin on top of them. He considered grabbing some food, as well, but figured he could get that later on the road. He slung the bags over his shoulders, walked out the front door, locked it, and headed for the stairway.

He looked at his watch. *Nine o'clock.* He made a mental calculation and figured he would be through with his business at the bank by ten at the latest and on the interstate by ten forty-five. Should have no problem with being in downtown Mobile by noon as he had planned. He was anxious to get going, and figured to skip breakfast and instead get lunch during his meeting with his source, then pick up dinner somewhere in Gulfport and take it to the motel. *That'll take care of today*, he thought. *One day at a time, Jack. One day at a time.* A familiar phrase popped in his head; he wasn't sure where it came from and had meant to find out where but never bothered to do so. It had served him quite well in the past and would again for now, and that was all that mattered. *Don't worry about tomorrow. Worry about today; it has enough problems of its own.*

***

Jack pulled out of the apartment complex, made a right onto the busy four-lane road, and felt the warmth of the midmorning sun streaming through the driver-side window. He drove south on the broad avenue, passing through several lights, finally stopping at the intersection with Cervantes Street. He couldn't help but notice the HOT DOUGHNUTS neon sign flashing at the Krispy Kreme on the far corner. It was tempting, but he knew he'd need something more substantial and let the thought pass.

When the light changed he cruised down the sloping hill to the traffic light at Gregory Street; he made a quick right and followed it into the downtown area. He turned left onto Palafox, and pulled into a parking space just opposite the Bank of Pensacola. He turned off the ignition, grabbed an empty brown leather briefcase from the back seat, pressed the LOCK button on the door, and got out. He waited for the oncoming traffic to clear the first two lanes, passed beneath the tall palm trees that lined the grassy median in the street, and crossed the final two lanes in front of the bank.

He entered the lobby of the bank, went over to the large counter that sat in the middle, quickly filled out a withdrawal slip, then turned and walked up to a very attractive brunette seated at the second teller's window. He smiled at her. *My God, she's beautiful*, he thought. *Must be new. I would definitely remember seeing her before.* He slid the withdrawal slip across the counter toward her.

The teller picked up the slip and looked at Jack. "Good morning, sir. How are you today?" she asked.

"Fine, just fine," Jack replied. He noticed she wore no rings on her left hand. *That's good.* He glanced at the nameplate that sat on the counter in front of her. *Nancy Richardson.* "I don't remember seeing you here before, Nancy."

She smiled demurely at him. "I've only been working here part time and just started full time last week."

Jack held his gaze upon her. She nervously looked down at the form, then back up at Jack. "Mr. Brantley, this is quite a substantial amount of cash you are requesting. Would you like that in the form of a cashier's check instead?"

"No, Nancy, I would not. I need it in cash. That's not a problem, is it? I mean, I know I have the funds available in my account. I wouldn't think it's a problem."

"No, sir, it's not. It's just that I don't have that amount of cash in my drawer. If you'll excuse me for a few minutes, I'll get the bank manager to handle it," she replied.

Jack stood at the window and watched her walk to the manager's office and knock on the door. A moment later she emerged, followed by a man in a black suit. Jack remembered meeting him when he first opened his account, but never saw him any other time he was at the bank. He couldn't for the life of him remember the man's name. Didn't matter. All he wanted to do was to get his money and be on his way. The man came to the teller's window opposite Jack.

"Good morning, Mr. Brantley," he said to Jack. "I'm Scott Andrews, the bank manager. Nancy has informed me of your request for a withdrawal today. She has also told me you want it in cash, not in the form of a cashier's check. I can do that for you, of course, although I strongly suggest that a check for that amount would be much safer than carrying such a large amount of cash."

"Look, Mr. Andrews, I don't think that should be a concern of yours. First, it's *my* money. Second, the funds should be made available to me in whatever form I wish. And third, you don't need to worry about my safety. I know how to take care of myself."

Jack noticed Nancy was listening very intently to the conversation and that she was looking directly at him. He wondered if she was as interested in him as he was in her, but told himself, *Maybe another time.*

"Very well, Mr. Brantley. I'll handle the transaction personally. If you'll wait right here, I'll get the necessary funds. I'll need your identification, for the bank's records, of course. I'm sure you'll understand."

"No problem," Jack said as he reached for his wallet. He pulled out the license bearing his own name. He wondered for a moment if he should have set up the account under one of his aliases, but so far it had not been a problem for him. *Too late to worry about that now,* he thought. The bank manager examined the license closely and then returned it to Jack.

"I'll be back in a moment, Mr. Brantley," Scott Andrews said. Jack placed the brown leather briefcase on the counter in front of Nancy's window and waited for the bank manager to return with the cash. He glanced down at his watch. *Not quite ten o'clock. Still okay, still on schedule,* he thought. *Man, I wish I wasn't in a such hurry to leave town.* He looked at the brunette teller once again. *I'd love to ask her out to lunch today.*

***

An hour later Jack crossed Mobile Bay on Interstate 10 and took the exit for the Bankhead Tunnel. He emerged from the tunnel onto Government Street and followed it for a few blocks until he saw the sign for North Jackson on his right. He signaled to turn, made a quick right, and drove through the intersection of Conti, then Dauphin, and spotted Jake's Bar and Grille on his left. He pulled into the parking lot, found an empty space, and turned off the engine. He glanced at his watch. *Eleven thirty.* He had a half hour to spare and figured he'd go in, have a beer, and look over the menu while he waited.

He recalled that it had taken most of yesterday afternoon on the phone to locate the accountant's office and set up a lunch meeting with him today. Jack planned to extract the information he was seeking on his client from him over a couple of drinks and lunch. He opened the briefcase, counted out twenty one-hundred-dollar bills, and placed them in an envelope and put the envelope back in the briefcase with the rest of the money. *The sniveling little weasel,* Jack thought. *If it's bad information, I'll track him down at his office one day and put a bullet in his head.* He grabbed the briefcase, got out of the Camaro, and headed toward the front door of Jake's.

***

After the bespectacled accountant had talked at length with Jack over a couple of beers and a superb lunch of rib eye steaks, loaded baked potatoes, and house salads, Jack reminded him of the dire consequences of providing false information. The little man assured Jack it was completely accurate and that the client they both worked for would never know where it originated. Satisfied with that response, Jack passed him the envelope and picked up the check the waitress laid on the table. The accountant thanked him for the lunch and Jack watched him walk out of Jake's.

Jack figured to hang around at the bar for another couple of beers and listen to the honky-tonk blaring from the jukebox in the corner. There was no need to rush now that he had the needed information; armed with it—and what he had it the trunk of his Camaro—he could take his time now. He had eight thousand dollars in the briefcase for necessary expenses and whatever—or whomever—he needed to buy. Added to that he had more than enough time for the short drive down I-10 to Gulfport.

It was nearly four-thirty when Jack Brantley pulled out of the parking lot at Jake's and drove back to Government Street. He found his way back to the interstate and was soon westbound again. It wasn't long before the lunch and the beers began working on him, making him not only drowsy but also in need of a bathroom. He pulled off the interstate at the Mississippi Welcome Center for the much-needed break.

Jack was soon back on the interstate, and forty-five minutes later he spotted the sign that read, "Gulfport/Beaches Next Exit." The sun was approaching the horizon, splashing the low clouds in the western sky with a brilliant touch of pink and purple and orange. He glanced at his watch. *Six o'clock.* As he moved over to the far-right lane, a couple of television advertisements came to mind. *Perfect ending to a perfect day. It doesn't get any better than this.*

He entered the exit ramp and slowed as he approached the intersection with the highway ahead. He waited for a couple of cars to pass to clear the intersection and accelerated quickly to turn left onto Highway 49. He spotted a sign just ahead on his right that told him he was inside the city limits and that the beaches were just ahead. He wouldn't be going downtown or to the shore; his business and concerns were far from there.

He passed a Burger King on his right and the image of Randy and Billy in the parking lot at the one in Moss Point flashed briefly in his mind. He wondered why he was thinking of them now, as this was a completely different exit and they wouldn't be found around here. Maybe it was just his antennae going up, warning him to get focused again. To be alert for other jerks like them. *You never know what, or who, you might encounter,* he thought.

He soon spotted a Kentucky Fried Chicken sign on his left. There wasn't much else around the exit—the Waffle House up ahead would take care of breakfast tomorrow morning. He turned into the parking lot of the KFC and pulled up to the drive-through menu. He placed his order, pulled up to the window, and handed a twenty to the teenage girl at the window. She returned his change and the bag containing two dinner boxes and handed him two drinks. He placed the bag on the seat next to him, the drinks in the center console, and pulled away. He hated going back to this run-of-the-mill fast-food diet he so often found on the road, especially after today's lunch. *The colonel's original recipe will just have to do for tonight,* he thought.

Jack pulled up to the exit sign, waited for the passing traffic to clear, and turned left onto Highway 49 for a hundred feet or so and then made a right turn into the parking lot of the Best Western Motel. He drove past the main lobby on his left and continued toward the end of the long wing that extended from the office. He turned left at the end of the building and drove around to it the other side. He spotted his room number and pulled into a parking space in front of it and turned off the ignition. He grabbed the drinks and the bag containing the dinners, picked up the briefcase and the duffel bag containing the weapons from the back seat, and got out of the car and locked the driver's side door. He noted the DO NOT DISTURB sign was still hanging on the motel room door and smiled. He inserted the key into the door lock, turned the handle, and stepped inside, quickly closing the door behind him.

"Jack, so good to see you again!" Father Edward Brennan said as he arose from the bed he was lying on. He walked to the television set, turned the volume down, and added, "I see you stopped to pick up some food. God Bless you, my son. To coin a well-worn phrase, I'm so hungry I could eat a horse!"

"Well, Padre, I hope a chicken dinner and a Pepsi will suffice," Jack replied.

"It will do just fine, Jack, just fine," Father Brennan said. "Here, let me help you with those things."

CHAPTER 11

Jack left Father Brennan to fuss over the take-out dinners and drinks and went back to his car to bring in the remaining bags and his other belongings. He laid everything on the top of his bed. He left the room once more, this time to move the Camaro to the end of the lot, down and away from the building that contained his and the priest's room. He parked next to the motel's enclosed dumpster, hoping it would be less noticeable there in the darkened corner of the parking lot. He walked back to the room, closed and locked the door, and slid the safety chain in its slot. *Lot of good that's really going to do*, he thought. *If they were to find us here and get the door unlocked, that chain won't do a bit of good.* It was a force of habit, and habits comforted Jack Brantley.

He was concerned, also, if he and Father Brennan were tracked down, whoever was sent to finish the job he refused to do would find another way in anyway. He remembered doing that very thing, when he was on one of his last assignments with the CIA. His target had locked himself in his room on the ground floor of an old Austrian inn and he had tried repeatedly breaking down the barricaded door. Unsuccessful in his attempt to get in, Jack told himself there was more than one way to skin a cat. He got in his Jetta and drove it through the door, pushing the bed and table jammed against it out of the way. He remembered getting out of the car that was now halfway in the room, putting two well-placed shots in the man's chest, adding his signature finale to the forehead, getting back in the car, and simply backing out of the room and driving off thinking, *Well, that was interesting.* Tossing the keys on the nightstand next to his bed, he proceeded to the bathroom and emptied his very full bladder. He washed his hands and was drying them with a towel when he stepped back into the small room and noticed that Father Brennan had set out the dinner boxes, drink cups, plastic ware, and the napkins on the small table in the corner of the room and had turned on the floor lamp next to the table. He saw the priest sitting on the edge of his bed, not at the table, with his eyes seemingly transfixed on the television set.

"So nice of you to set the table, Father," Jack said. "Gives the place a real homey feel, don't you think? I trust your accommodations have been suitable and that you've slept well these past two nights?"

Father Brennan turned toward Jack. "Yes, Jack, everything's been fine," he replied. "I've been quite comfortable, as a matter-of-fact. And I'm certainly glad you showed up with this dinner. I ran out of the food you left for me after I ate last night, so I missed both breakfast and lunch altogether today. It's just as well. A little fasting is good for the body as well as the soul, you know."

"So you stayed in this room, even though you were out of food?" Jack asked.

"Yes, Jack, I did," Father Brennan replied. "Just as you asked. Actually, as you *told* me to. I have to admit it was difficult, but I saw how serious you were about my staying out of sight, so I did just that."

"What did you do to pass the time, Father?"

"Besides watching a lot of television, I found a Gideon's Bible in the nightstand there and reread Matthew, Luke, and John. And several of the Psalms. My favorite is the twenty-third; I read it several times. Considering all that's transpired, it's quite appropriate. You know—walking through the valley of the shadow of death and all."

"That's nice, Father. Real nice," Jack said. "Has anyone come to the door? Has anything out of the ordinary happened since I left you here yesterday morning?"

"I heard the housekeeping staff pass by a couple of times, that's all. They didn't come in, of course, not with that DO NOT DISTURB sign you left hanging on the doorknob. No one else came calling after you left, if that's what you're asking." Father Brennan paused a moment, then added, "Jack, are you sure you need to go to all this trouble? Hiding me in this motel room, keeping me out of sight like this?"

"Yes, I do, Padre. I can't express to you enough the seriousness of this whole situation. Some very unpleasant men will be sent our way. I don't know when they'll come, but they *will* come sooner or later. It's only a matter of time until they track us down wherever we are."

"It seems then I've become the object of another manhunt, doesn't it, Jack?" Father Brennan turned up the volume of the television set when the commercial ended and the news came back on. "It's one thing having the police out looking for me, and now you tell me 'some very unpleasant men' want to find me, as well."

"*Us*, Father. They'll be after both of us. Me, for not doing the hit on you, and you, because the man who hired me still wants the job done."

"No matter how many times I've heard that phrase said on all those police shows on television, I never thought it would apply to *me*. I still don't understand why there's this 'hit' on me in the first place, Jack." He paused and turned toward the television screen. "See, there I am *again*. It looks like I've become somewhat famous, wouldn't you say?"

"Yeah, Padre, you're what's known in the media as a 'celebrity figure.' Keep it up and you'll outshine the archbishop. Maybe even the Pope himself."

"Jack, no one will surpass His Eminence, and I have no intention of drawing any further attention away from the work my beloved archbishop is doing in New Orleans," Father Brennan replied. He paused, then added, "This seems so unnecessary, and it's taking me away from performing my duties, you know."

Jack noticed the anxious, concerned look on the priest's face as he listened to the voice-over on the television set. He turned his own attention to the screen and saw the familiar photo of Father Brennan and the phone number of the New Orleans Police Department below it.

"As of this broadcast," the male voice stated, "police have not revealed to us anything further about the disappearance of Father Edward Brennan of the Archdiocese of New Orleans. As we have been reporting, Father Brennan has been missing since late Tuesday afternoon and there's still no word as to his current location. Father Brennan, the much-beloved associate parish priest at the Sacred Heart of Jesus Catholic Church on West St. Charles Street, is perhaps better known throughout the Business and Warehouse Districts of downtown New Orleans for his work at the Catholic Charities Office on Baronne Street. As we have been reporting, he was last seen. . ."

"Well, well, Padre," Jack interrupted, "you have indeed become 'the man of the hour,' haven't you?"

"Jack, I really can do without all this notoriety, all this fuss and bother, you know," the priest replied. "I'd really like to get back to my normal duties and routine. But I'm quite certain you have other plans for me, don't you?"

"Yes, I do, Padre. I'm thinking about taking you up to Hattiesburg right after breakfast and our checking out of here tomorrow morning. It's only a couple of hours up Highway 49. I'm certain the police and my ex-client won't think to look for you there. They'll all be focusing their attention up and down the coast instead in their search for you and me."

"Jack, I am forever in your debt for what you're doing for me, but I have my responsibilities to attend to and I can't stay hidden forever, you know. How long can this go on? Sooner or later they'll find me—and you, and then what?"

"I know you have your obligations, Father," Jack replied, "but I have a good reason for keeping you alive. At the appropriate time, I plan to have you resurface back in New Orleans, but until then you've got to trust me. I'll keep us one step ahead of the police until I'm ready to let them find you. I'm not too worried about them. It's my ex-client and his brother I'm more concerned with. I'm sure my failure to take you out is not sitting well with them, and I know they'll be sending somebody else to finish you off. They'll come after me next."

"Well, I'm sure they don't appreciate your taking their money and not carrying out their wishes, but you chose not to do it for a reason, Jack. You could have easily pulled the trigger on that gun of yours two days ago and could have accomplished what you say you were hired to do, but you didn't. Instead you brought me here, to these *lovely* accommodations, and made sure I was all right before you left yesterday. For all that I am eternally grateful. But this goes far beyond the two of us, Jack. You see, there is a higher power at work here. You and I both know that God's hand is all over this."

"Father, I really don't have time for this. I'm hungry and tired and want to get some sleep. We have a busy day ahead of us tomorrow, so let's just eat and turn in, okay?"

"All right, Jack, we'll eat. But we have a lot to talk about tomorrow. You must tell me why you were hired to kill me in the first place, and why you are now so intent on keeping me alive. Then you will listen to my side of the story, of what *I* must do despite all your best-laid plans."

Father Brennan walked over to the small table, pulled out a chair, and sat down. Unfolding a napkin and placing it on his lap, he looked over at Jack.

"Young man, would you care to join me in this bountiful feast the Lord has been so gracious to provide us with?"

Jack walked to the table, sat down, and opened the box in front of him.

"You mean what *I* have provided, don't you, Father?" he countered.

Not waiting for a reply, Jack pulled out the containers of mashed potatoes and coleslaw from his box and placed them on the table. He pulled out a drumstick from the box and proceeded to lift it to his mouth. He looked up and noticed Father Brennan was staring at him.

"What?" he asked.

"Excuse me, young man," Father Brennan said, "will you be so kind as to wait a moment before you indulge yourself?" The priest then folded his hands and closed his eyes. "Bless us, O Lord. . ." he began.

Jack sheepishly returned the drumstick to the opened box and bowed his head. He kept his eyes open, watching the priest as he prayed.

"...for these, thy gifts, which we are about to receive. From thy bounty, through Christ our Lord. Amen."

Father Brennan opened his eyes, and looked over at Jack.

"Well go ahead, young man," the priest said. "Eat your dinner, before it gets any colder."

***

After they had finished eating, Jack walked over to his bedside and sat down on the edge of the bed. He watched Father Brennan throw the empty boxes and cups in the trash and wipe down the top of the table with a wet washcloth he had gotten from the bathroom. Jack unzipped the duffel bag containing the shotgun and his .45. He pulled the pistol out of the bag and placed it in the drawer of the nightstand next to his bed. He then pulled the shotgun out of the bag and laid it on the floor beneath the bed. He looked up and saw that Father Brennan was watching him intently.

"That's an awful lot of firepower you have there, Jack," the priest stated. "Do you really need all that?"

"I told you, Father, some very serious-minded people will be out looking for us. I'm not sure if they're going to find us tonight, or tomorrow for that matter. But eventually they *will* find us. And I plan to be ready for them when they do. So, if you will, Father, let's both get some sleep. As I said before, we have a very busy day ahead of us tomorrow."

"Very well, young man," Father Brennan said, holding the Gideon's Bible in his hand. "But if you don't mind, I have a little more reading I'd like to get done. I found some stationery this lovely motel provided and I'd like to make a few notes, also. I'll try not to disturb you."

"Suit yourself, Padre," Jack replied. "Good night," he added as he turned the light off above him.

"Good night, Jack," Father Brennan said. "Sleep well."

CHAPTER 12

Jack woke from a deep, dreamless sleep as the first rays of light filtered through the drapes covering the motel room window. He slowly opened his eyes and looked around the room before remembering where he was and why he was there. He heard Father Brennan in the shower, singing at the top of his lungs. He laid there, forcing his brain to begin functioning again, and listened to the lyrics and the tune of the priest's song. It seemed vaguely familiar, something he had heard a long time ago. Was it on the radio, or on a television show? *Sure isn't on any of my cassettes*, he thought. He laid there in his bed, struggling to recognize the song. *One thing's for certain. It's certainly not ZZ Top.*

He continued to listen. "Moon river, wider than a mile. I'm crossing you in style, some day." *That sounds like something mom and dad would have listened to.* "Two drifters, off to see the world. There's such a lot of world to see." *What the heck is that he's singing?* he wondered.

He reached over to the nightstand and opened the drawer. He picked up a pack of cigarettes lying next to the .45, extracted one of them, and lit it. He leaned back against the pillow behind him and drew in the smoke. He held it in his lungs for a moment, exhaled, and listened to the lyrics of a second song coming from the bathroom. "L.A.'s fine but it ain't home. New York's home but it ain't mine no more." *Got that one!* he thought. *Neil Diamond.* He listened as the priest continued singing. "I am I said, to no one there. . ." *Still don't know who sang the first one. I guess I'll have to ask Father Brennan when he gets out. If he ever gets out.*

Jack continued to lie in the bed and the priest remained in the shower. He finished his cigarette, waiting for the song to end, hoping the priest would emerge soon from the bathroom. *I need to get in there soon*, he thought. *Gotta pee like a racehorse.*

He thought he heard the water stop, and started to get up from his bed. However, the water in the shower kept running, and Jack heard Father Brennan launch into a third song. He sighed and shook his head from side to side, then laid back down in the bed and listened to the lyrics of the new song. "Song sung blue, everybody knows one." Despite the need to pee, he was beginning to enjoy this. He thought of an old TV game show from the fifties called *What's My Line?* If this game went on the air it could be called *What's My Tune?* "Song sung, blue, every garden grows one."

That one's easy, he thought. *Neil Diamond again.* A few minutes later, Father Brennan sang yet another tune. "Hands, touching hands. Reaching out, touching you, touching me. Sweet Caroline." *Well, at least I know he likes Neil Diamond.*

Jack laid in the bed, figuring it would be a few more minutes before the priest would finish this new song, *hopefully* dry off, and get dressed and relinquish ownership of the bathroom to him. He reached over and extracted yet another cigarette from the pack. He lit it, leaned back against the pillow, but the urgency to get in there was growing stronger by the minute. *As much as I'd like to hear "Solitary Man" next, Padre, you have to get out of there. I GOTTA GO!*

Jack finished his cigarette and the shower still ran. He sat up in the bed, rubbed his hand through his hair, and walked over and stood at the bathroom door. "Hey, Father, how much longer are you gonna be in there?" he yelled through the closed door. "I really need to get in. I have to go pee something fierce."

"Good morning, Jack!" Father Brennan shouted back. "I won't be much longer. But don't mind me. Come in if your business is all that urgent."

"Uh, that would be kinda awkward, don't you think?" Jack replied.

Father Brennan yelled through the closed door again. "Not at all, my friend. When I was in the seminary there was one small bathroom on my floor, and six of us had to share it. I think it will be okay if you come in. I promise I won't look."

Jack hesitated a moment, but his bladder wouldn't permit him to wait any longer. *The heck with it*, he thought as he opened the door and quickly lifted the lid to the toilet.

Father Brennan continued to regale Jack with the story of his days at the seminary. "You see, Jack, the way it worked was one of us would be in the shower, one would be standing over the toilet, while another was shaving at the sink. The first three of us would rotate places and we'd all finish and head back to our rooms to get dressed while the other three took their turns in the bathroom. Modesty was a virtue we couldn't afford to practice at that time, not if we wanted to get downstairs for breakfast and then make it to our classes on time."

Jack hovered over the toilet and replied, "Sounds like you had it a little better than I did when I was in basic training. Uncle Sam threw thirty of us together in my barracks. All we had available to us was this wide-open bathroom. Not a whole lot of privacy there, that was for sure."

"We do what we have to do in life sometimes, don't we, Jack?" Father Brennan said.

"Well, Padre, as long as we're on such an intimate and friendly basis, as soon as I'm done here I'll throw on my jeans and shirt and head over to the Waffle House and get us some breakfast. What can I get for you?"

Father Brennan turned off the water to the shower. Jack heard him going through the motions of drying off with a towel behind the curtain. "Now, don't go to any trouble, Jack. But if it's all the same to you, I'll take two scrambled eggs, a side of hash browns, two slices of unbuttered toast, some strawberry jelly, and a tall cup of orange juice. I'm famished, and that should do quite nicely."

"Jeez, Father," Jack replied. "Maybe I'd better get a pen and a piece of paper to write it all down. Can I get you any sausage to go with that order?"

"No, thank you all the same," Father Brennan replied. "I've given that up. Permanently. Gave up the butter, as well. It's bad for the arteries, you know. Oh, and get me a cup of coffee, will you, Jack? I can't quite give up the caffeine just yet. No sugar, mind you. Just be sure to get a few packs of creamer."

"That powdered stuff? Isn't that just as bad for you as sausage?"

"You have a point there, Jack. Ask them for some half-and-half. If they don't have it, get a cup of milk instead. That'll be okay for the coffee, I suppose."

"I really *should* write this down, Padre. It's so early in the morning, and I'm half asleep as it is. I might not remember it all."

"If you wait a few minutes, Jack, I'll get dressed and come with you. We can eat there; I could certainly use a break from the confines of this room."

"No can do, Padre," Jack said. "I can't let you be seen right now. Just sit tight and maybe somehow, someway, I'll manage to get the order right. I'll be back." He turned and walked out the door.

"Try not to be gone too long, Jack. And by the way, it's your turn to say the blessing."

Jack closed the door to the bathroom. "I'll leave the praying to you, Father," he said quietly.

"What?" the priest yelled through the closed door. "I didn't quite catch that."

"Nothing, Father. Nothing at all," Jack yelled back through the door. "I'll be back shortly."

***

"That was a wonderful breakfast, Jack," Father Brennan praised as he emptied the contents of one of the small containers of half-and-half into the Styrofoam cup in front of him. "Thank you."

"Hey, no problem at all, Father," Jack replied. "Although when I looked at the bill, I was glad I went by the bank yesterday morning and held it up. Figured I needed lots of cash to cover your room and board."

"I thought your profession was knocking off people, not banks."

"Just kidding, Padre. I did take out a lot of money, but I did it the proper way."

"Well, Jack, that's a relief. I appreciate all the trouble you're going through on my behalf."

"It's the least I could do, Father," Jack assured. "By the way, I enjoyed listening to you belt out a few tunes in the shower this morning."

"I'm sorry if my singing woke you, Jack," Father Brennan said. "I wasn't too loud, was I?"

"At first you weren't, but the more you sang the louder you got. Thank God there wasn't anyone next door to us on either side. They'd have complained, that's for sure."

"I always try to keep it low when I sing, but you're right. I've been told I have a pretty good voice, but the same people who tell me that also tell me I'm rather boisterous when I sing. I know I must have woken you. I'm truly sorry I didn't let you sleep longer."

"That's okay, Padre. The sun was coming in through the window and that's what really woke me up. It always does. I usually don't sleep well anyway. I won't go into detail with you as to why, but suffice it to say a lot of bad dreams don't help very much." Jack paused a moment, then said, "Funny, I don't remember dreaming at all last night. It felt good. I feel like I got a good night's sleep for once. Then I woke up and heard you singing."

"Was it okay, or was it really dreadful, Jack?"

"It was actually okay, Father. Like I said, it was kind of fun listening to you. You do a pretty good impression of Neil Diamond."

"Well, he is one of my favorite singers, Jack."

"I especially liked 'Sweet Caroline,' Father. It took me back in time a little bit. I heard him sing it at a concert once. Woburn Abbey in England, back in seventy-seven. I had some down time from the CIA, there was this girl I had the hots for... Oops! Sorry about that, Padre...there was this girl I especially liked and I was lucky enough to get two tickets for us. I'll never forget that concert. Fifty-five thousand British fans packed in there! That producer, William Friedkin, had his cameras there, filming the performance. It was great."

"And your date, how did she like it?"

"Get this, Father. Her name was Caroline! She was thrilled when he played 'Sweet Caroline.' She said it was 'her song' and she was convinced he was singing it just for her. I knew better, of course."

"Didn't she know it was written about Caroline Kennedy, when she was a little girl?" Father Brennan asked.

"Apparently not. I wasn't about to spoil it for her, so I played along and we sang along. I'm not a huge fan of his; I'm more of a rock-and-roll kind of guy, but it was great watching him perform."

"It sounds as though you and Caroline had a great evening."

"We did, Father, we certainly did. What happened after the concert— well, if I told you it would have to be in the confessional booth." Jack smiled like the Cheshire Cat from *Alice in Wonderland* and quickly changed the subject. "Did you ever get a chance to see him, Padre? You being a fan of his and all, I hope you've seen him live at least once. Nothing quite like his shows. They say he feeds off the energy of the crowd. He certainly did that night at the Abbey."

"I did, once," Father Brennan replied. "I got to see him at one of his Winter Garden Theater performances in New York City in nineteen seventy-two. I was in the city attending some special training sessions the Church provided for its Catholic charities administrators, and a few of the other priests and I went to see him. He is quite a talented man. And energetic, too, as you pointed out."

"Well, now that we've established our mutual admiration for Neil Diamond, I'd like to ask you who else you like to listen to. What I'm trying to find out is the name of that first song I heard you singing in the shower this morning. The one about the moon and the river. I know I've heard it before, and it's driving me nuts trying to figure it out. What was the name of it and who sang it?"

"That was 'Moon River' by Andy Williams," Father Brennan replied. "A classic from the early sixties. A bit before your time, though, wasn't it?"

"Yeah, just a bit," Jack replied. "Good to know the answer, Padre. I thought it sounded familiar. I think my mom and dad actually owned some of his albums."

"They'll be worth a lot of money someday, Jack. Tell them to hang on to them."

"Not possible, Father. They're dead now. But if I ever see my younger brother Richard again, I'll be sure to tell him. He was the only one of us who wanted their record collection, so he has it. I got Dad's guns. I was the only one interested in them."

"I'm sorry to hear they've passed away, Jack. I hope they were faithful servants of God and the Church."

"Oh, they were, Father. You couldn't have found two people more devoted to God, the Church, or to each other. All that church stuff wasn't for me, but it was for them. I grew up with it at St. Michael's School, and went to Mass and all that, just to make them happy, I suppose. Once I left for the army I never attended another Mass." Jack paused, then looked at Father Brennan. "I suppose that makes me an awful person in your eyes, you being a priest and all."

"I don't think of you that way, Jack," Father Brennan replied.

"Well, with what I've done, I don't think I have a chance at all, Father."

"I'm sorry you feel that way," Father Brennan replied. "But if I may—I know this is going to come across as a lecture, and believe me it's not intended to be—I do believe God allows us the freedom to choose what we wish, and you have chosen this particular path you are on in your life right now. It's not a good one—you know from your upbringing it's not. But do I believe He will forgive you and allow you to return to Him if you wish—"

Jack quickly interrupted him. "You're right, Father, it does sound like a lecture, and I don't care to go there with you on the subject right now. Maybe some other time, but not right now. Okay?"

"As you wish, Jack, as you wish."

"That *is* my wish, Father," Jack sternly said. "Now, enough about me. You said last night you had some questions for me, some things you wanted to know. Let's talk about you then. More specifically, about what I found out about you and why I was hired to kill you."

"I'm very interested in what you have to tell me about your client, his brother, and the reason why they wanted me killed. But before you do, promise me we'll get back around to talking about you, your parents, and your family. Most importantly, about your relationship with God."

"I'll agree to talking to you about me and the family stuff, Padre, because there's something there to talk about. The 'God' stuff—well, there's nothing going on between Him and me right now so there's really nothing there to talk about. Okay?"

"Then by all means go ahead and tell me about this man who hired you, and what you will do to stop your replacements. From the guns I've seen you display, I'm quite certain it won't be a pleasant experience for them."

"No, Father, it won't," Jack said.

"Before we get started, however, I need to visit that bathroom over there," Father Brennan said, pointing to the open door. "Excuse me, will you, Jack? I promise I won't belong. If you'll pardon the pun, I'm just dying to find out."

CHAPTER 13

Father Brennan emerged from the bathroom and found Jack sitting in the worn, overstuffed chair in the far corner of the room. The light hanging over the small table had been turned off, and the thick, heavy curtains over the window had been drawn so that almost no sunlight entered the room. Jack had turned the chair so that it faced the front door of the room. He held a cigarette in his left hand; a thin plume of smoke drifted slowly from it toward the ceiling.

"You know, those things are going to kill you one day," Father Brennan stated. "They took my father's life. He was just fifty-two when he died from lung cancer."

"That's a very real possibility for me, too, Padre," Jack replied. "It's a bad habit, I know, and I've tried to quit a number of times. But hey, we're all going to die someday, and I'm figuring it will either be these cigarettes or someone's bullet that'll do me in."

"That's not a healthy philosophy of life to harbor, Jack. It's a bit fatalistic, wouldn't you say?" The priest paused before adding, "And why are you sitting over there in the dark?"

"Just another habit of mine, Father," Jack replied. "Unlike these cigarettes, this one's a pretty good one to have in my profession."

Father Brennan saw that Jack had his hand resting palm down on the right arm of the chair; beneath Jack's hand was the gun he had pointed at him Tuesday afternoon. It was the same gun he had seen Jack place in the nightstand last night. The sight of it was enough to send a chill down his spine again. When that had passed, he understood what Jack meant. A scene from an old episode of *Columbo* came to mind; in it a brooding, menacing assassin—*just like Jack over there*, he thought—sat alone in a similarly darkened room, waiting patiently for his intended target to walk through the door. Even though the central theme of the popular television show dealt with someone's murder each week, he loved watching it. He considered *Columbo* a "thinking man's" show. He made it a point to keep his schedule free when it was on so he wouldn't have to miss an episode.

"I suppose some habits are hard to break, aren't they?" Father Brennan said as he sat down in one of the chairs at the table, adjusting it so he could face Jack.

"Some are a little harder than others," Jack replied. He took a final draw from the cigarette and mashed the end of it in the ashtray next to him on the other arm of the chair. He turned his head and looked over at the priest sitting next to him. "Well, Father, there's no sense in beating around the bush, so I'll get right to the point," he began. "After I made a few phone calls when I got back to my apartment Wednesday afternoon, I set up a meeting with the accountant of my ex-client at a bar and grille in Mobile yesterday afternoon. For a reasonable amount of money—and a lunch at my expense, as well—I was able to get some very interesting information from the little snitch. It seems my client's brother paid a visit to your church recently and *you*, Father Brennan, were the lucky one who got to hear his confession. In-between bites of his steak and baked potato, the little weasel told me he had overheard a conversation between his client and his client's brother; he had stopped by their office one afternoon and apparently neither of them knew he was outside their office door listening. He said the younger brother sounded really nervous as he told his older brother he had killed one of their business rivals over a woman. He said he heard the elder one reply, 'So what, Gino? Just as well that it happened anyway. That's one less competitor we'll have to deal with.' Then came the kicker, Father. The accountant said it nearly floored him when he heard it. It wasn't just *some* woman—it was Gino's *wife!* The accountant told me he heard Gino tell his brother he had walked into their bedroom and caught his naked wife and her equally naked lover in a rather passionate embrace. He heard Gino say, 'Sal, I had no choice but to pull out my .38 and shoot him. Then I looked at my wife, shook my head, and walked out the door.'"

Father Brennan sat motionless at the table next to Jack; one side of his brain listening to him, the other lost in thought, recalling the confession he had heard that Saturday afternoon at Sacred Heart. He remembered sitting in his chair in the darkened confessional, meditating and grieving over the sins he had just heard and that he had just absolved, waiting patiently for the next person to enter the adjacent booth and pull back the small screen that separated them. Before long another penitent entered the confessional; he heard the small window slide back and he focused his attention on the male voice coming through the thin curtain separating them. *How I wish I had never heard that man's confession*, he thought. It was one he'd just as soon forget, but unfortunately he couldn't. The words had been forever etched into his memory.

"Bless me, Father, for I have sinned," the husky male voice intoned. "It's been four weeks since my last confession."

"Go ahead, my son," Father Brennan said to the voice.

"Father, I have committed the following sins in the past few weeks: I have lied on several occasions to my wife and to my business partners, I have taken God's name in vain at least seven times, I have not attended Mass the past two Sundays, and. . ." The voice paused.

"Go ahead, my son. Continue," Father Brennan said.

". . .Father, most of all, I am truly sorry for committing the sin of murder."

". . .Because of that, Father Brennan, you became a marked man," Jack concluded. "And so, yours truly was given the contract to take you out, Father. The envelope with the money came with specific instructions for me to find and kill Father Edward Brennan of the Sacred Heart of Jesus Catholic Church in New Orleans. At the time, I didn't know why. Didn't care, either. It wasn't any of my business anyway. I was paid twenty-five grand for the job, Father. Half up front, the other half upon completion. That was all the reason I needed at the time. So I tracked you down and found you. Forced you at gunpoint to come with me. I even picked out a very secluded, swampy area across the lake up near Mandeville to do the job, and planned to leave your body for the gators to feast on while I headed back across the causeway and down into the Quarter for an evening of relaxation." He paused, his voice choking as he continued and said, "But then I saw something in you I haven't seen in others in a very long time. At first, I thought it was just courage that I saw, but I knew it was far more than that. What I saw was absolute *fearlessness* in your eyes, Father. There I was, with my forty-five aimed right at your heart; I'm ready to pull the trigger and blow you away and I just couldn't do it. I must admit it now, Father, it was a lousy thing I was about to do, but when I saw how you weren't afraid to die, something just got to me. All I can say, Padre, is there was no way I was going to go through with it after that. I just didn't have the stomach for it anymore."

Jack waited for the priest to launch into a tirade at him. After all, he had it coming to him, with what he had just said. But Father Brennan just sat there, grim-faced, staring vacantly past Jack to the other side of the room.

"Father, did you hear what I just said?" Jack asked. "That's the long and short of it. The reason why I was supposed to kill you. And the reason why I didn't." He paused before adding, "At least now you know the full story." He pulled a cigarette out of his pack, lit it, inhaled deeply, and exhaled very slowly. The cloud of smoke seemed to hover in the air around him before it dissipated.

Father Brennan turned slightly and looked at Jack. "Yes, Jack, I heard what you said. And I appreciate your telling me. When you said you saw courage in me—well, let me tell you I was terrified; I was truly expecting to die and I feared for my life. But I quickly realized if you did kill me I'd be in the presence of God the very next moment, and that comforted me greatly. That was the 'fearlessness' you say you saw in me. It wasn't a lack of fear that you saw, Jack. There was a lot of it floating under the surface.

The fearlessness you say you saw in my eyes was from the calming presence of the Holy Spirit." He paused, then added, "And a verse from the Bible popped into my head, where Paul wrote 'For me, to live is Christ, but to die is gain.' How could I be fearful after that, knowing I'd be with my Heavenly Father for all eternity?"

"I don't know, Father. That may work for you, but it doesn't for me. Not with what I've seen and done in my lifetime. There's way too much water under the bridge for me to think like that. I'm afraid I'm headed in the opposite direction when I kick the bucket."

"That's because of the unconfessed sin in your life, Jack. Although you won't admit it, I can see it troubles you greatly. Sin is what separates us from God, and it must be confessed. No sin is so great that God won't forgive us of it. And when He does, He remembers it no more. All you have to do is confess them. Do that, Jack, and heaven awaits you." He paused before adding, "Don't, and hell awaits. It's your choice. It's really that simple."

"I've heard all that before, Father. Funny thing is, I used to believe it, too. But I don't anymore. I can't." Jack paused, then said, "Take murder, for instance. That's one of the 'mortal sins' in the eyes of the Church. This Gino fella, he goes and commits it by killing his wife's lover. He feels guilty about it, so he comes to you and confesses it. You absolve him of his sin, dispense some form of penance on him, and tell him, 'Go in peace, my son. God has forgiven you.' And so he's off the hook from going to hell for it? Excuse me, Father, but he's still a murderer as far as society is concerned. He still has a price to pay, don't you think? Maybe it needs to be made public what he did, so he can answer to the law for it."

"What that man said to me in the confessional was private, between him and me and God. No one else was supposed to know what went on in there. He should *never* have told his brother. And this accountant you said you talked to—this modern-day 'Judas Iscariot'—how much did he *really gain* in passing along this information to you?"

"It cost me a couple of grand, Father. But I really didn't mind paying it."

"I'm not talking about the money, Jack. I'm talking about the principle of the matter. Some things that are said in confidence should remain that way. Is there no shame left in this world?"

"I suppose not, Father. The love of money. . . Hey, I'm just as guilty as the next guy. I guess I'm really no better than Gino, or that little jerk in Mobile, I suppose."

"Is that a confession I'm hearing, Jack?" Father Brennan asked.

"No, Father, it's not."

"Maybe the beginning of one then? It's time for you to turn away from this path you're on. Time to put all this behind you, Jack. Please ask God for His forgiveness, before it's too late. Return to Him."

"What, like that Prodigal Son in the Bible? I don't see that happening to me, Father. Like I said, too much water under the bridge. Besides, I couldn't afford it." After a moment, he added, "I think I've run out of time, too."

"What do you mean by that, Jack? There's nothing that has to be paid anymore. It's been paid by Jesus Christ; by what he did on the cross."

"I'm not talking about that, Father," Jack replied. "I'd be giving up too much money if I quit this business. I make a darn good living doing what I do."

"Some things are more important in life than making money, Jack."

"I figured that's what you'd say, Father. Money may not be the key to happiness, but it sure keeps the wolves at bay."

"And the thing you said about time, Jack. What made you bring that up?"

Jack extinguished the cigarette, threw the butt in the half-filled ashtray, and said, "I don't know, Father. I've got this feeling—had it for a while now—that I've pushed the envelope a bit too hard. If I were a cat, I'd be on my ninth life right now. I'm kind of fatalistic, aren't I?"

He didn't wait for the priest to respond; he simply stood up and said, "Excuse me for a minute or two, will you Father? It's time I paid a little visit to that bathroom over there." He paused, then turned back to the priest. "Keep an eye on that for me, will you?" he said, pointing to the .45 lying on the arm of the chair. "It's loaded, so don't go messing around with it."

"Trust me, Jack. I wouldn't dare touch it. I wish you wouldn't, either."

***

Jack returned from his bathroom break, sat back down in the chair, and lit another cigarette. Father Brennan frowned at him; Jack glanced down at the cigarette in his hand and then looked up at the priest.

"What, Padre? Is the smoke bothering you or something?"

"It is, but I'll survive. I'm worried you won't, Jack. How many packs a day do you smoke?"

"One, sometimes two. I know, I know. I've read the warning from the surgeon general. Maybe I'll get lucky, and a bullet will kill me before these things do."

"Yes, I remember you telling me that. It's really not funny, you know."

"I never said it was. I'm serious, Father. I just don't think it's in the cards for me to live a long, healthy life. I'm too much of a realist. There's not a lengthy life expectancy in my line of business. Not too many of us live to retirement age."

"You know it doesn't have to be like that, Jack. What concerns me most is your flippancy about it all. Surely you're not as indifferent about your life as you're making it sound. Every life has value, Jack. God made us in—"

"Yeah, yeah, I know. 'He made us in His image, to know Him, to love Him and to serve Him.' Blah, blah, blah. Remember, Father, I had all that shoved down my throat for eighteen years. First by Mom and Dad, then the priests and the nuns at St. Michaels's back home in Pensacola. But then God goes and lets me down." He paused to take another drag on the cigarette. "Please, Father, I don't need any of it from you, too. Okay?"

"Jack, you can be antagonistic toward me, but why God? What happened to you to make you so—so *disappointed* with Him?"

"If only you knew, Padre. If only you knew. Let's just say I've seen so much evil in this life that I believe God just doesn't care anymore. I know what you're thinking and I agree—I know I'm responsible for some of that evil out there with what I do for a living. I still believe He's out there and all, but I just don't think He takes too much of an interest in what we do down here anymore. I think He's about as jaded as I am." He paused before adding, "Life isn't what it's cracked up to be, you know. Sometimes I think the alternative to living might not be so bad after all."

"Jack, I know you don't want me to preach to you—"

"You're darn right, Father," Jack interrupted. "So don't."

"Okay, but allow me to say one more thing and I'll then shut up. I'll do my best to not say another word on the subject after this. God does indeed care for us, and He takes what we do *very* seriously, Jack. So seriously, in fact, that He sent His one and only Son to show us His love and mercy and grace. To forgive us for our failures, so that one day we can be with Him for all eternity. Please take that seriously and think about what happens after this life has ended and we stand before Him. We *will* stand before Him, Jack, and account for our lives here on this earth. The alternative to eternal life is eternal death, separation from Him and His love." He paused, then added, "Do me a favor and just think on that a little, will you?"

"Maybe I will, Father. Then again, maybe I won't. Now, if you will, Padre—"

"Yes, Jack. I'll bite my tongue," Father Brennan said. He wanted to continue, but he could sense it was best to change the subject. For the time being, at least. "Now then, let's get back to this 'hit' that was placed on me. I'm puzzled by it and I'm trying to make some sense of it all. I mean, what would be the point? I wouldn't have said anything to anyone. I can *never* reveal what was told to me in the confessional. When I became a priest one of my vows was that I would never break the Seal of the Confessional. Not even if my life depended upon it."

"I don't think they saw it that way, Father. I think they got worried you *would* reveal the confession to the police. They're running scared right now. That's why I came into the picture." He paused, then said, "And so, here I am."

"Yes, here you are. Looks like you were the one handpicked for the job, Jack. Chosen by—"

"Yeah, I was chosen by them all right," Jack interjected. "I had done a couple of jobs for these guys in the past, and they threw a lot of cash at me to take this one. Now that I think about it, I'm a little upset with myself for considering going through with it in the first place. I'm more upset with myself than I am with them. But that'll change soon enough. When my replacements find us, I'm afraid I won't be in a very good mood, Father." He paused, then said, "I won't be rolling the red carpet out for them when they arrive, that's for sure."

"I agree you were chosen by those men for the job, but more importantly, I believe you were chosen by God for it, as well. And there's one other thing for you to consider, Jack. Just as those men made a choice in picking you to come after me, *you* made a choice of your own—you chose *not* to go through with it. That decision was not just because you— what was it you said?—you 'didn't have the stomach for it.' It was actually your conscience bothering you, and that's where the Holy Spirit enters the picture."

"I thought we weren't going to bring any of that back into this conversation. I thought you agreed to that, Father."

"No, Jack, I didn't really agree to it. You said you didn't want me to 'preach' anymore. So I'm not preaching, Jack. I'm just talking to you as your friend. Think of it as my way of offering you some very friendly advice. My opinion on some of life's most important matters. Do you remember what I said to you last night? God's hand is all over this, Jack. He brought the two of us together for a reason. He had a purpose in doing so. I believe with all my heart He placed us in each other's paths for a specific reason, so that good things will result. Goodness comes out of encounters such as these, and whether you believe it or not, Jack, something good will come of all this. All because of a choice you made."

"Sorry, Father, I still think of that as preaching. If not, then it sure sounds more like a lecture than just your opinion and friendly advice. Don't get me wrong. I appreciate your concern for me, but like I said before, tell that to the kids at that Catholic high school down the road from your church. Better yet, save all this 'good and evil'/'God's will'/'God's mercy and grace' discussion for one of those Theology 101 classes at Loyola, will you? I'm more interested in what Real Life 101 taught me."

"And what is that, Jack?"

"That life's a bitch, Father. A genuine struggle where only the strong survive."

"That's a little harsh, Jack. *I* wouldn't put it quite that way. Life *is* hard. No doubt about it. It has its trials, I agree. But it's often during those trials that we need Him the most. Things have happened to cause you to turn your back on Him, but He hasn't turned His back on you, Jack. He's right where He's always been. You've just got to quit your wandering away from Him and return to Him."

"There you go with that Prodigal Son business again."

"Sorry, Jack. I just can't help it. It's a favorite of mine. I've given many a sermon in my time based on that parable."

"I don't doubt it, Padre. Not for a minute. But let's change the subject, okay? I know that may grieve you a little, but we have other things to think about and discuss. First and foremost, I've got to think about saving your skin. And mine. I've kept you here at this motel long enough and need to move you today before they find us."

"So what's next?" Father Brennan asked.

"Like I said last night, we're off to Hattiesburg in a little while," Jack replied. "I'll check you into a motel there. I know this one is lacking, so I'll go all out and find one with a kitchenette in the room. One of those extended-stay kinds of places. Get you a couple of days' worth of food, some more clothes. Get you out of that priest outfit of yours, so you're less noticeable."

"And what then?" Father Brennan asked. "Move me again? It has to stop some time, Jack. I can't agree to staying hidden much longer."

"I know, Father," Jack said. "I wouldn't expect you to. I promise you I won't let it go any longer than it has to. While I have you squirreled away

I'll be setting things up. Getting ready for them when they make their move. You just have to let me handle it my way."

"I hope you know what you're doing, young man," Father Brennan said. "I know you're a hard man and won't let them get the best of you. It's just all this moving around, keeping me hidden and away from my duties." He paused momentarily before adding, "I don't like it, I'll have you know."

"I didn't think you would, Padre. I wouldn't like it myself, if the shoe were on the other foot. But like it or not, I'm just planning to keep one step ahead of everybody until I'm ready for all of them."

"One might think you're running scared, Jack. Not me, of course, but others might."

"That would be a mistake, Father. A big mistake. No, what I'm doing is merely mimicking the actions of the tiger that lives in the jungle."

"What are you talking about, Jack?"

"Apparently you've never heard the ancient Chinese proverb, Father. 'The tiger fights, then runs away. And lives to fight another day.'"

"No, Jack, I haven't heard that one. There's one I know, not quite as ancient. Maybe you've heard it. It's from the Bible. I hope they are not too familiar with it."

"What's that, Father?"

"'Seek and ye shall find,'" the priest replied, grim-faced as he said it.

"That's a good one, Padre. But I don't think we should worry too much," Jack said reassuringly. "I don't think anybody hired to take my place to come after you would be referred to as a Bible student. We just need to be careful and everything will be all right."

"So we'll be checking out of this lovely motel," Father Brennan said, "and we'll drive north for a couple of hours, and check into another just like it?"

"No, Father. We'll upgrade. I told you, I'll try to find an extended-stay hotel, one that has some amenities like a refrigerator and a coffee maker. Maybe even a small stove. All the comforts of home. I'll make sure it has a Gideon's Bible, and better stationery for you to write your notes on. I'll keep you there until it's not safe anymore. Then I'll move you again."

"It sounds like I will definitely miss saying this Sunday's Mass, doesn't it, Jack?"

"I'm afraid so, Padre. But if you'll let me do this my way, I may have you back in front of your congregation at Sacred Heart the following week. You can use some of what's happening to you right now in one of those sermons of yours. You'll really have something to tell them, won't you?"

"Yes, I suppose I will," Father Brennan said. "I'll leave out the part about the younger brother's confession, of course. Everything else—well, I guess that's 'fair game,' as they say." He paused, then said, "I still don't like this. The fact that it's going to take several more days. I don't like knowing so many of my parishioners will be worried about me."

"Well, Father, I can assure you of a couple of things," Jack said. "First, that they will be praying for you. And second, they'll be real surprised—and happy—to see you again. So bear with me and just do as I say and we'll come out of this all right."

"I still don't like the idea of being gone so long, Jack. It's just too long, you know."

"Look, Father, I'm really sorry about that, but it *has* to be this way," Jack insisted. "So it's off to Hattiesburg for a few days. From there, if we have to, I'll move you over to Alexandria, then on down to Baton Rouge. Wherever we are, wherever we end up, if all goes according to my plan we'll return to New Orleans and you can safely show your face again. Hopefully everybody with a stake in this will be looking for you along the coast, and it'll give me the time I need to be looking for them, as well. And preparing for what's bound to happen because of the encounter."

"It seems you've thought this through quite carefully, haven't you, Jack? You're quite experienced in this kind of thing, aren't you?" He paused, then added, "It seems I have very little to say in the matter, doesn't it?"

"To answer you, Father, I have had to do this on more than one occasion. And, no, you don't have much of a say in this. I know what's best for both of us."

"Then my choices are quite limited, aren't they, Jack?"

"Yes, Father Brennan, they are," Jack replied as he headed toward the bathroom. He stopped when he got to the door and turned back toward the priest. "We're burning daylight, Father, and right now, I need a shower and a shave. When I'm done, we'll be on our way."

Father Brennan replied, "I'm still not convinced of the need for all of this—"

Jack cut him off. "Don't make me say it again, Father. We *will* be on our way, just as soon as I'm finished cleaning up. Trust me when I tell you this, Father—we'll live to fight another day. I promise you that."

CHAPTER 14

Jack had just gotten out of the shower, dried off, and was standing in front of the mirror studying his reflection. A shower usually revived him, but this one failed to do so. He just felt so. . .*tired*. He attributed it to the stress he was under, dealing with the fall out from his decision to not kill the priest and from thinking about what was ahead of him. He'd handled far worse than this, and he knew it. But this seemed different, and he wasn't quite sure why.

He really hated to be so tyrannical with Father Brennan, but he knew it was for the best to be like that with him. He knew the priest didn't like being cooped up in a motel room going on three days, and he was reasonably certain the he was not going to cooperate fully when the three days turned into a week or more. He had calculated the risks and figured the odds were in his favor. He had gone over the different scenarios in his mind and concluded this was the best hand he had left to play. Maybe the only one. Despite any further objections he was certain to receive, the plan would remain just as it was.

He went over the details in his mind, just to reassure himself it was indeed a good plan that he had come up with. The first stop would be in Hattiesburg; the last would be in New Orleans. Those were etched in stone. He would not deviate from them no matter what the priest would say during their drive north on Highway 49. The stops in-between, well, he could be a little more flexible, so long as he felt they contributed to the end result of flushing out his ex-client, that idiot brother of his, and the guns for hire they sent to kill the priest and himself. No matter what, the ultimate goal was to drive into New Orleans after having 'stirred the pot' a while and see what came out of it.

He knew he had an arsenal big enough for what he had planned, enough firepower to cause some real excitement wherever he'd find them—or where they'd find him. He'd have both the .45 and the 12-gauge pump loaded and within immediate reach; he had plenty of reserve ammunition if it was necessary. He also planned to move the .38 Smith & Wesson from the trunk of the Camaro to the glove compartment—easy enough to pull it out from there if he needed it, as well, he reasoned. There was no doubt that Father Brennan wanted desperately to return to his church in New Orleans, perhaps even head over to the Catholic Charities Office on Baronne Street to resume his duties there, but Jack figured the ex-client and his brother would have both places staked out and Father Brennan would be a sitting duck if he showed at either one. *It's got to be my way*, he thought. *That's just the way it is.* He wrapped himself in the towel, grabbed another one to finish drying his hair, and walked out the door of the bathroom to check on Father Brennan. There wasn't really anything for the priest to pack, so Jack thought, *He ought to be ready to go.*

"Father, I hope you've gotten everything ready—not that you have a lot to begin with. . ." Jack stopped in mid-sentence when he realized there was no one in the room but himself. "Dammit, Father," he said as he went to the front door and placed his hand on the knob, only to realize the futility of opening the door—he knew the priest was long gone, and he wasn't dressed to go chasing after him right now anyway. "Dammit!" he yelled as he walked back to the bathroom.

***

Jack quickly dressed and gathered together his gear and laid it all on his bed. He had already thought about what he'd do next—pack up, check out at the front desk, and ask the clerk there if he or she knew anything about the priest's whereabouts. It was a longshot, but he had to start somewhere. *Besides, I might get lucky,* he thought. *Father Brennan wouldn't have wanted to use the phone in the room with me being around and may have gone to the lobby to use the one there to call the police, maybe even somebody from the church, to come get him. Can't blame him for that. I'd have done the same thing.* Jack started packing his gear into his duffel bags. He was upset with himself that he had lost control of the situation. It hadn't happened before, and he didn't like the feeling. He was also upset with himself for overlooking the possibility the priest would do just what he did—head out the door and never look back. He had no one to blame; he merely assumed the priest would be in such fear for his life that he'd allow Jack to control the situation and go along with what was planned.

As he was packing, something odd struck him. After looking around for a few seconds, he saw what it was in the room that made him feel that way. He looked over and noticed that Father Brennan had pulled up the sheets and the bedspread on his bed; it didn't surprise him at all that he had done that. What caught his attention was the Gideon's Bible that was propped against one of the pillows on the bed, along with a folded piece of paper with Jack's name written on the outside. He picked it up, unfolded it, and read it.

Jack,

It is late Thursday night as I am writing this, and by the time you find it tomorrow morning I hope I'll have found someone to help me so I can begin the process of getting back where I belong—back to my parish in New Orleans. Do not worry, my friend. I will not mention you to the police or to my superiors at the archdiocese. When they ask why I was in Gulfport, I will offer them some excuse about my desire to "get away from it all," or something like that, and that somehow, I ended up here. I'll figure out what else to say as I go along. Yes, Jack, it will be a lie, and I hope the Good Lord will forgive me for that small sin. Rest assured I will not reveal your whereabouts or your participation in this matter. Thank you for your concern for my well-being, Jack. I hope we'll have a chance to talk before I leave. In case we don't, please know I harbor no ill will toward you, and I absolve you of any wrongdoing in this matter. I simply must get back to where I am needed, and as always, I will place my life in God's hands. If He wishes that I live, then I will do so and will continue His work back in New Orleans. If not, then the men who you say are looking for me will undoubtedly find me and, I am certain, will no doubt kill me, just as you have also said. Either way it goes, Jack, God wins. I am reminded of a verse from Philippians (1:21) where Apostle Paul said, "For to me, to live is Christ and to die is gain."

May God be with you, my friend.
Father Edward Brennan

P.S. I have a special request of you. Please read the several passages of Scripture I have marked for you in this Bible. I've numbered them for a reason, Jack, and hope you will take the time to read them in that order and reflect on them. My prayer is that you will seek God's forgiveness and return to Him.

"Father, you really don't know what you're getting yourself into," Jack said aloud as he picked up the Bible. He noted the several pieces of paper protruding from it that marked the passages the priest selected. He sat down on the edge of the bed and examined the book. *Can't bother with reading them right now,* he thought as he folded the note from the priest and placed it inside the cover. *I'll read them some other time, Padre. Right now, I've got to figure out what to do about your situation.*

***

Jack quickly finished packing and put everything in the Camaro. He checked the room, saw that he'd left nothing, and closed the door. He walked to his car, got in, and started the engine. *Let's see how much of a head start you've gotten, Padre.* He drove around to the front of the motel, parked beside the lobby, turned off the ignition, got out, and walked inside to the front desk. The lone female clerk looked up at him from whatever it was she was working on in front of her.

"Good morning, sir" she said. "How may I help you?"

"Just checking out," Jack replied as he handed her the key to his room.

The clerk checked the number against the registration log in front of her. "I hope your stay with us was satisfactory, Mr. Pittman," she said while making out the final receipt for him. She stamped it PAID IN FULL. "Is there anything else I can help you with today?"

"Yes, as a matter-of-fact, there is," Jack replied. "I was wondering if you've seen a man in a black suit come in here this morning. He's white, middle-aged, kind of tall—six-one or so—balding."

"Yeah, I did," she said. "And boy, oh boy was it ever exciting! Not when he first walked in, but toward the end it sure was."

So he did come here, Jack thought. He needed to find out what Father Brennan did while he was here, and hopefully, where he went afterward, as well. He had to think quickly and come up with something to get the desk clerk to tell him. A few lies would be told, but so what? He was good at telling them, and she looked like the type who'd listen to anything he had to say.

"What do you mean?" Jack asked her. "My brother's not *that* exciting."

"Your brother?" the clerk asked. "The priest is your brother?"

"What priest? My brother's just a boring accountant," Jack said. "I told him to meet me here after I checked out this morning. I'm supposed to drive him back to Mobile today. But then you go and mention something about a priest." He paused, then added, "Now that you've gotten my curiosity aroused, what exactly is going on?"

"I'm sorry. I assumed you were looking for the priest," she said. "The whole thing was kinda weird anyway. I mean, in walks this man, kind of like you described: tall, balding, wearing a black suit. But he looked like some sort of minister, the way he was dressed. You know, with that white-collar thing and the all-black suit. And then it came to me—he was the priest on the news! The one that went missing in New Orleans, the one that everyone's been looking for. He asked if there was a pay phone in here. I told him there wasn't one in here but there was one outside. Then he fumbled through his pockets and said he didn't have any money to make a call anyway. Next thing he does is ask me if he could he use the desk phone for a call over to New Orleans. I said I couldn't let him do that, because of the long-distance charges. Motel rules and all, you know. He said, 'Sure, I understand.'"

"Yes, I'm certain you have your rules to follow."

"You bet I do. I'd get in some serious trouble really quick for something like that. But then, to top it off—I'm sorry, Mr. Pittman. Here you are looking for your brother and I'm going on and on about the priest instead."

"Hey, that's all right," Jack said. "My brother can wait. Tell me more about this priest. You said it got exciting toward the end. What happened?"

"Well, then he asked if there was a Catholic church nearby, and I told him there was. St. Anthony's is just down the street, I said. Then he said, 'That's perfect. I'm sure they'll help me get back to New Orleans.' He asked how far it was to the church. I told him it was about a mile or so down on the right. He said something like, 'That's not too far. I'll walk.' Then he turned and headed out the door!"

"He *walked* to the church?" Jack asked.

"He was about to, but I wasn't gonna let him do that. I ran right after him and told him it was way too dangerous to be walking down Highway 49," she replied. "All that traffic—he could get run over! So I told him to come back in here and I'd call the Gulfport police and get them to pick him up. I told him I was pretty sure they'd take him to the church, if he asked them and told them that's where he needed to go. He said not to bother them, he didn't want to get them involved, and could I just call a taxi instead? I told him, 'Father, the police have been looking for you and I think they'll be wanting to see you first.' And he just sort of shrugged and said, 'Okay, I'll wait for them.' So I called them and the next thing I know an officer shows up, asks him a few questions, and off they go in a patrol car."

"Wow, that does sound exciting," Jack said. "Bet it made your day, didn't it?"

She smiled as she said, "Yeah, it sure did."

"Well, I'm glad he's okay," Jack said. "Anyway, like I said, the fella I'm looking for is my older brother. He was supposed to be dropped off at this motel and come inside and wait for me here in the lobby. I haven't seen him for such a long time and, like I said, the plan was for us to meet here and I'd drive him back to Mobile. Catch up on things during the drive, that sort of thing." He paused and looked around the lobby. "Obviously he's not here."

"Like I said, the only man in a black suit to come through here this morning was that priest. And he's long gone by now."

The desk phone rang and the clerk placed her hand on the receiver. Before she picked it up to answer it, she said, "He seemed like a nice-enough priest. I sure hope he made it to St. Anthony's like he wanted."

Jack nodded his head to thank her for her information and turned toward the front door of the lobby. There were two places to begin looking for the priest—St. Anthony's Catholic Church and the nearest Gulfport Police Department precinct. He knew going to either of them was not an option, and as he walked out the door he thought, *I guess it's on to Plan B then.* The trouble was, he didn't have a Plan B. He'd knew he'd have to come up with one in a hurry.

***

Jack left the motel parking lot and turned north onto Highway 49. He began to formulate an alternate plan, but found it difficult to focus on it—he was still upset at himself for letting his guard down back at the motel room. He assumed the priest would just sit tight and wait while he showered and dressed. He should have known better. Father Brennan was possibly at St. Anthony's, but more than likely he was taken elsewhere for some answers before a call would be placed to the archdiocese office in New Orleans. But it didn't matter. Either way he looked at it, the priest was off-limits now as he was in the hands of the Gulfport Police Department. Jack knew there would be numerous questions the priest would have to answer, first from the Gulfport officer who picked him up at the motel and then there would undoubtedly be many more thrown at him by the priests and staff at St. Anthony's, assuming he made it that far.

He also thought about what it would be like for Father Brennan when he made it back to New Orleans. *The poor guy makes it through the first round only to face round two.* He imagined the priest facing some burly detective with the New Orleans Police Department before someone at the archdiocese office got hold of him. *Might even be the archbishop himself who'd do the grilling, wanting to get to the bottom of it.*

Jack began to think more clearly now that he had gotten past his anger at himself for being so careless back in the motel room. *All that questioning is bound to take a few hours,* he figured. *At least the rest of today. Maybe even most of tomorrow morning. That should give me enough time to do what I need to do.*

***

About a half mile north of the motel Jack spotted the two large green signs that were attached to the side of the interstate bridge that crossed over the highway: EAST MOBILE/PENSACOLA RIGHT LANE and WEST NEW ORLEANS LEFT LANE. He eased into the left one and stopped under the overhanging light, waiting for the oncoming traffic to clear before making his turn onto the westbound ramp. As soon as he entered the on-ramp he quickly accelerated and merged with the flow of traffic that was westbound on the interstate.

After a few minutes, he read a smaller green sign that stood on the right shoulder of the highway: NEW ORLEANS 70. He calculated he would be on the eastern edge of the city in about an hour. How long it would take him to cross the city and make his way out to the west side, to the church on St. Charles, on a Friday afternoon—well, that was anybody's guess. However long it took, Plan B was set in motion: get to the far end of the Garden District, maybe even the Uptown area depending on what was available, and get a room for the night; grab some dinner at a nearby restaurant or café; head over afterward to the Sacred Heart Church and park somewhere nearby and conduct surveillance for the evening. The next day, as well, if necessary. He'd scope *everything* out and leave nothing to chance. *Don't know if the priest will show up tonight or tomorrow, but he'll show up sooner or later*, he thought. *And so will the goons Sal and Gino are sending.*

Jack continued driving toward New Orleans, thinking, *And I'll be waiting for them. Tonight, tomorrow. It doesn't matter. I'll be waiting.*

PART THREE

RECONCILED

CHAPTER 15

Jack had been driving a little over half an hour on I-10 since leaving Gulfport and was preoccupied with pressing the SEEK button on the radio, trying to find a station with some current news about Father Brennan. None of the stations in Gulfport or Biloxi were reporting anything, so he continued to press the button on the radio, trying to locate a station out of Slidell or New Orleans instead. It tuned in on a classic rock station—probably one out of New Orleans, he figured—and he recognized the Doors' "Light My Fire" blasting over the airwaves. He turned up the volume and found himself distracted for a few minutes as the song played through. He was willing to listen to anything this afternoon, from the Allman Brothers to ZZ Top and almost anything else in between, just to take his mind off his troubles and pass the time. *Maybe they'll play some Led Zeppelin, some Santana, a little Rolling Stones,* he thought. *That would help a lot along this God-forsaken stretch of the interstate.* Foreigner was up next instead, and when they sang, "My mind is racing, but my body's in the lead; tonight's the night, I'm gonna push it to the limit," he thought it was quite appropriate considering the circumstances he faced.

An orange-colored hatchback flashed by him on his left and abruptly moved over into his lane a few feet in front of him. Jack pressed hard on the brake pedal to back off and avoid a likely rear-end collision with the vehicle. He felt his anger beginning to rise, but he quickly let it pass. Any other time he might be tempted to chase the idiot in the car, do the same to him, and initiate a confrontation, but he had far more important things on his mind. *First things first, Jack,* he thought. *Focus on what you have to do. Find out what's going on with Father Brennan.* He pressed the SEEK button again and kept trying to find a news station coming out of the Big Easy, but he didn't have any luck finding one. Finally, he caught the tail end of a report coming out of a station in Slidell and he listened intently.

"...Our source at the Gulfport Police Department told us Father Brennan was to be picked up later today by a representative from the Archdiocese of New Orleans and returned to his residence at the Sacred Heart Church on St. Charles Avenue some time this evening. Officially the department wouldn't reveal any details of the disappearance of Father Brennan, nor would they tell us where he had been for the past few days. We contacted the Office of the Archdiocese of New Orleans but a spokesman there declined to reveal specific details, as well. His only comment was, and I quote, 'It is certainly good news for the many residents of New Orleans that Father Brennan has been found unharmed and in good spirits.' And now, for your local weather. It will continue to be sunny and warm this afternoon. . ."

Jack turned down the volume on the radio. *Glad to hear he's okay,* he thought. *Problem is, if I'm hearing all this, so are Sal and Gino and the goons they've hired.* He imagined the two brothers ordering his replacements to take care of the priest first, then him. He knew he had it coming to him for what he did—actually, for what he didn't do—and he knew they would not give up until their objectives had been accomplished. After all, he had taken twelve and a half grand of Sal and Gino's money. His refusal to fulfill his obligation meant two things: first, he was out the other twelve five, of course, and secondly, Sal and Gino were highly ticked off at him. But he was okay with it all; he found it quite surprising that he was thinking this way. *Something about the priest must be rubbing off on me,* he thought.

***

Jack drew closer to the Mississippi/Louisiana border on I-10 and was bouncing a couple of ideas around in his head, trying to deal with the problem he faced—how best to protect Father Brennan now that he was back in the public eye. He needed a specific plan, and he had to think of one quickly. He knew he had to make it foolproof. The priest's life—and his—hinged upon what he would end up doing.

He was beginning to come up with a plan—a pretty good one, he thought—when the need to find a restroom arose. He crossed the state line into Louisiana and saw the sign for the Welcome Center. He exited the interstate and slowed his approach to the building, looking for an empty parking space. It appeared crowded this morning; the parking spaces directly in front of the building were filled, so he drove farther down, past them until he could find an available spot. He turned off the ignition, but didn't get out right away. Instead, he sat in the Camaro for a few minutes, thinking through the rest of the plan. *It just might work*, he thought. *But so many things have to fall in place for me to pull it off.*

He glanced down at the seat next to him and saw the Bible lying there. He picked it up, opened it, and pulled out Father Brennan's letter. He read through it again, folded it carefully when he was done, and placed it back in the Bible. He looked at the cover of the book and noted the Gideon's label at the bottom. He knew that they placed them in hotel and motel rooms across the country in the hope they would be picked up and read; he wondered if the organization counted on some of them being removed, to be read later. *There you go, Jack. Feeling that "Catholic guilt trip" again.* He smiled at the thought. *Well, if it is a sin for keeping it, it's just one of those small ones. One of those "venial sins." Can't get into too much trouble over them, if I remember correctly.*

He got out of the car, locked it behind him, and stepped onto the sidewalk leading to the building. He really needed to find that restroom soon, and was relieved when he spotted the sign directing him to the left side of the building. After his brief visit there, he sought to put his newly formed plan in motion. The first step meant finding a phone. If there was one here, great. If not, then he'd just drive to the next exit and find one at a gas station or fast-food restaurant.

He had been thinking how best to handle the situation now that the priest was heading back to Sacred Heart tonight. He thought Father Brennan would want to make the Catholic Charities Office his first stop if it was during normal business hours. But the announcer on the radio mentioned Father Brennan would be at the residence later this evening, which meant the Catholic Charities Office would be closed and Father Brennan would have to go to the church instead. That being the case, Jack planned to go to the rectory next to the church. That was step two. He figured Father Brennan would get dropped off and stay there for the rest of the night. He was counting on that. Step three was where it got a little tricky, a little more. . . *Don't get too far ahead of yourself,* he thought. *Find the phone. Make the call first.*

He walked into the visitor's center and quickly scanned the interior. He spotted a pay phone hanging on the wall near the exit to the building. He was glad it was far enough from the main counter so no one would listen in on his call. He walked over to it, picked up the receiver, and punched 0. After a moment the operator came on.

"May I help you?" a female voice asked.

"Operator, I'd like to place a call to the New Orleans Police Department," Jack said.

"That would be long distance, sir," she replied. "You'll need to deposit two dollars to begin the call."

"No problem," Jack replied as he reached into his pocket for some loose change. He pulled out a couple of quarters and a dime. He chided himself for not having enough change for the call.

"I don't have enough change on me," he told her. "I'll have to find someone here to break a five. May take a while. I really need to make this call, but I guess I'll have to call back later."

"I'm sorry for the inconvenience," she said. Then she added, "Sir, is this an emergency call you're placing?"

Jack thought about it for a moment before responding. *It may not be now, but it might be soon enough.* "Yes, ma'am, as a matter-of-fact it could end up being one."

"One moment," came the reply on the other end. "I'll see if someone at the department will accept the charges. May I tell them the nature of the call?"

Jack thought she sounded like she'd been an operator for a while and knew the ropes; maybe one who could really help him. "Just tell them I have some vital information regarding Father Edward Brennan," Jack stated. "They'll recognize the name. Tell them I was involved in his disappearance and now there are some people who are looking for him who want to see him dead."

"You mean the priest who went missing?" the operator gasped. There was an awkward moment of silence on the line before she spoke again. "Sir, is this a. . .?"

"I know what you're going to say. No, ma'am, this is *not* a hoax. I'm quite serious. I really need to get through to someone at the police department before something tragic happens to Father Brennan."

"I know someone who works there," the operator said. "He's a desk sergeant. I think he'll be interested in talking to you, but I'm just not sure if he's on duty right now. I'm going to put you on hold while I try to find out."

Jack held on, waiting for the operator to return. *I'm glad she recognized the name of the priest,* he thought. *She should have. He's been all over the news.* He hoped she would find this "someone" she knew at the NOPD who would accept the call and be willing to listen to him and take him seriously. If not, then he'd think of something else. He knew this was a long shot, but he had to play it out anyway. It was a matter of life and death.

A couple of minutes later the operator returned on the line. "Sir, I have Sergeant Michael Gillette of the New Orleans Police Department on the line. Officer Gillette, will you accept the charges for this call?"

"I will," came the reply.

"Go ahead, sir," the operator said to Jack.

"Sergeant Gillette, do you recognize the names Richard Pittman and Raymond Patterson?" Jack asked.

"I do. In fact, the entire New Orleans Police Department is quite familiar with those names," the voice on the other end replied.

"As am I, Sergeant," Jack said. "Very familiar. I'm quite close to each of them, as a matter-of-fact. And I think you'll be *very* interested in what I have to say about them."

"Are you calling to report the whereabouts of these men? It would help tremendously if you can tell me where they are. We have APBs out on both of them. The NOPD has been looking for them for a few days now." There was a moment of silence on the line, then Gillette said, "The operator told me you have some information about the disappearance of the priest and that his life may be in danger. What exactly is your involvement in this matter?"

"To make a long story short, Sergeant, there was a hit placed on Father Brennan, and I'm the man who was hired to kill him. My name is Jack Brantley, but I'm also Richard Pittman and Raymond Patterson. I used those aliases when I was looking for the priest. Are you interested in me going into more detail?"

"I am," Sergeant Gillette replied. "I'm *very* interested. Please continue."

"I located Father Brennan in the Desire Projects Tuesday afternoon, at the apartment of his former housekeeper on Abundance Avenue, and I forced him to leave with me at gunpoint. But something strange happened to me afterward—it never happened to me before. I had a change of heart and refused to kill him. Just couldn't do it, you know what I'm sayin'? So I drove over to Gulfport and stashed him away in a motel for a couple of nights until I could figure out what to do next. I knew all this wouldn't sit too well with the men who hired me—I knew they'd get someone else to find him and kill him, then send someone after me."

"I'm sure they would," Sergeant Gillette said. "Are you looking to turn yourself in? Is that the reason for the call, Mr. Brantley?"

"No," Jack replied. "That's *not* the reason why I'm calling. I'm calling you because I'm more interested in protecting the priest. I'm counting on you to help me do that."

"And just how am I to assist you, Mr. Brantley?"

"By helping me protect him. I heard the news over a radio station out of Slidell a little while ago. And if I heard it, I'm sure my former employer, his brother, and the guys they hired to finish the job on the priest heard it, too. I had Father Brennan under my protective custody back in Gulfport, with plans to keep him under wraps until I could flush out the men I knew would be coming after him and me. But then the priest took off on me this morning. I knew where he was headed, or where he wanted to go anyway. Right back to his church. I also know that when he gets there, my replacements will be waiting. I need him placed under *your* protective custody now, Sergeant Gillette." He paused for added emphasis. "I'm sure you can understand the urgency of this situation."

"I can, Mr. Brantley," the voice on the other end said. "But I must advise you—you've probably figured it out anyway—I've had this call traced and we've located the phone you're calling from. A Louisiana State Trooper is en route as we speak. He should arrive at the I-10 Welcome Center very soon."

"It doesn't matter, Sergeant. When he gets here he won't find me at this phone. I'm headed into the city to see if I can find Father Brennan before those goons do. I want to see him come through this thing alive. They don't." Once again, he paused for added emphasis. "They're going to want to report back to my former employer that he's dead, and that they sent me packing along with him."

"What specifically do you want the New Orleans Police Department to do?"

"First, I want you to dispatch a couple of officers to the Sacred Heart Church out on St. Charles and a couple more to the Catholic Charities Office on Baronne Street. I'm thinking he will go straight to the church, but he might just want to stop by the Catholic Charities Office along the way. He'll go to one of the two and I'm afraid my former employer's new hit men will figure that, as well. They can split up and cover both places, but I can only be at one place at a time. I'd like to even up the odds a bit. Cover all bases, if you know what I mean. I'm hoping your men will get over to Baronne Street while I head for the church."

"I don't have the authority on this level to make that kind of call, Mr. Brantley," Sergeant Gillette said. "Let me get Detective Zach Goodman on the line so he can talk to you. He's been assigned to this case. Perhaps he can—"

Jack cut him off. "Quit stalling, Sergeant Gillette," he said. "I told you I won't be here when that trooper arrives. You can tell him he can find me at the church, if he's all that interested. I'm just counting on you to send some of your officers out to the charities office, like I ask. It'd be nice if you sent a couple of them to the church, as well, just for an added precaution." He paused, then said, "And there's one other thing, Sergeant Gillette. Radio the state police and tell them to have their trooper stop by the information desk here at the Welcome Center. I'll have an envelope waiting for him with some very interesting information in it on my ex-client and his brother. I'm sure you'll recognize their names, as well. Sal and Gino Russo."

"*Those two* hired you?" came the reply on the phone. "Yep," Jack answered. "I'm counting on your department, the state police, and the D.A. himself to put a little more pressure on them with what I'll leave behind. I've got a lot of details in there that should go a long way toward putting them away for quite a while. There's a little old lady at the counter here, handing out state maps to anybody who asks for one. Have the trooper see her for the envelope." He hung up the phone.

I hope he's going to do as I asked, Jack thought as he turned away from the phone and headed toward the information desk. *If he doesn't, then I'll do what I can. I just hope we're all not too late.*

***

Jack walked back to his car, got in, and turned the key in the ignition. He was backing out of his parking space when he looked in his rearview mirror and noticed that a Louisiana State Police car had pulled into the welcome center and braked to a halt in front of the entrance. *That was quick*, he thought as he watched the officer emerge from the vehicle and walk quickly toward the entrance. As he pulled forward toward the acceleration lane, the thought occurred to him that his plan might just work after all. *I'd like to see you come out of this without a scratch, Padre. And I'd like to see Sal and Gino nailed for this, and all the other stuff they've been involved in.*

***

As he pushed on toward the city, he knew from experience he'd soon be at the I-10/I-12 juncture; there, he'd make his usual slight turn to the left to follow Interstate 10 into New Orleans. The rest of his plan included getting off the interstate at the French Quarter exit, make his way over to Canal Street, turn toward the river, go down a few blocks, and pick up St. Charles. There would be a lot of traffic to contend with at that time of day; he had no choice but to get in the middle of it and then follow St. Charles out to the church on the west side. He wasn't certain what would take place after arrived, but he was counting on seeing at least one, maybe two, hit man waiting. He was just hoping to see a couple of uniformed officers from the NOPD there, as well.

He glanced at his watch and saw that it was approaching two o'clock. He realized he hadn't eaten since breakfast this morning, and hunger was gnawing at him now. His plan hadn't included a break for lunch, so he made an addendum to it. *I'll just get off at one of the Slidell exits*, he thought. *Go through a drive-thru there and grab something. Jump back on the interstate and eat along the way.*

He began thinking about what he would do once he got out to the edge of the Garden District where the church was located. *Get there, scope it out first. Then if everything's okay, I'll leave for a little while. I'll have to find a hotel nearby and check in, then get some dinner somewhere before heading back to the church to check everything out again.* He began to feel a bit anxious and he fought to control it. He knew what was causing it—it was the "what ifs." *What if my plan doesn't work? What if I fail and Father Brennan gets killed? What if. . .? Stop it, Jack,* he chided himself. *You can only do what you can.*

He glanced down at the Bible that lay on the seat next to him. He saw the pieces of paper protruding from the pages of the book and began thinking about what Father Brennan wrote in his letter. *I'll make a deal with you, Padre. If I can't sleep tonight, I'll go ahead and read them. After all these years, I may just open that book again after all. Curiosity may get the best of me. After all, what can it hurt?* He thought about the answer to that question. *A lot, really. Look what it did to that cat.*

CHAPTER 16

J ack pulled up to the Church of the Sacred Heart of Jesus at about five thirty in the afternoon. The parking lot next to the church was empty and he had plenty of spaces to choose from. He backed the Camaro into a spot that gave him a clear view of the front of the church, as well as the rectory next to it. He settled down in his seat, dreading the watching-and-waiting routine. From past experience he knew all too well this surveillance would likely spiral downward into boredom very quickly. He knew there was nothing much he could do about it, either; it came with the territory.

After two hours of observing only passing traffic on St. Charles he was reasonably certain nothing was going to happen for a while. He started the engine, pulled onto the street, and headed for the Pontchartrain Hotel. Mardi Gras week, which filled the hotels in and around New Orleans, had already come and gone and he thought he'd have no problem finding an available room there. If not, he'd simply drive closer to the city, maybe as far as Canal Street, to find a room for the night. He preferred to stay overnight in the Garden District and be as close to the church as possible, and as he entered the lobby of the Pontchartrain on St. Charles he was hoping he'd have to go no farther than this.

He walked up to the desk and rang for the night clerk. A young man, dressed in a freshly pressed, white long-sleeve shirt and a green vest was at the complimentary coffee and tea stand restocking it when he heard the bell. He quickly turned and walked toward the desk.

"Good evening, sir," he said as he walked behind the counter and faced Jack. "How may I be of assistance?"

"I'd like a room for the evening, first floor if it's available," Jack replied.

"I have two available rooms, both with king beds, but unfortunately they're on the fourth and fifth floors," the clerk stated. "One is smoking, on the fourth. The other is nonsmoking, on the fifth. Will either of those be sufficient?"

"I'll take the smoking on the fourth," Jack replied as he reached for his wallet in his back pocket. He had transferred some of the cash from the envelope inside his jacket to his wallet to avoid the risk of anyone spotting the .45 he was wearing underneath the jacket.

"If you'll fill this information out for me and provide me with your driver's license, we'll get started, sir," the clerk said as he handed Jack a registration form and pen.

Jack handed the man his license and opened his wallet. The clerk examined the license briefly and asked, "What form of payment would you like to make, Mr. Brantley?" Jack had thrown caution to the wind and was using his own name now. The cat was out of the bag, so there was no need to hide under an alias any longer.

"I'll pay in cash," Jack replied as he reached into his wallet and pulled out two crisp bills bearing the likeness of Benjamin Franklin. The clerk made out a receipt for Jack and handed it to him with the change and a key to his room. "If you'll give me a moment, Mr. Brantley, I'll call for a bellman to assist you with your luggage, and a valet to park your car for you."

"No need for that," Jack said. "I'm going to get some dinner and take care of a few things. I'll be back later tonight."

"Feel free to call on me when you are ready, sir," the clerk responded. "I'll have someone assist you then. Enjoy your dinner, and thank you for staying with us at the Pontchartrain."

***

Jack drove east along St. Charles until he found a small café nearby and parked in front of it. He was seated by the hostess at one of the outdoor tables, and when his waiter arrived, he placed an order for two bottles of Michelob, a plate of fried shrimp with a side of coleslaw, and a small bowl of jambalaya. When the waiter returned with it Jack ate ravenously, downing it all with the ice-cold beer from the bar. A gentle breeze stirred the humid night air and a faint scent of azaleas floated in with it, undoubtedly from one of the well-manicured lawns nearby. Jack thought about the events of the long day behind him and was tempted to hang around a while longer to relax and unwind with another beer or two. The waiter walked by and Jack considered ordering one, but decided against it; after all, it just wasn't in his plan. What *was* in the plan he had made for himself was to get back to the church and the adjacent rectory for a couple more hours of surveillance. *Just can't wait*, he thought. *Friday night in New Orleans, and I have to park my butt in front of a church.*

***

Jack drove slowly along the front of the church and the rectory, glancing at the front of both buildings as he did so. The church was darkened, and only a soft light shone through one of the first-floor windows of the rectory; they both appeared devoid of any signs of life. He pulled over to the curb, cut the engine, and slid the .45 out of the holster underneath his jacket. He laid it on the seat next to him and settled into his seat. From his vantage point he could clearly see the front of the priest's residence, as well as the front entrance to the church next to it. He glanced down at his watch. Nine forty-five. *I'll give it 'til midnight, maybe a little longer*, he thought. *Then I've got to get some shut-eye.*

***

The rest of the evening turned out to be nothing more than a long, boring Friday night that slipped slowly into Saturday morning. Jack was exhausted from the long day behind him; the more he thought about it, the more he realized it had turned out to be another one of those bone-weary, dead-tired, can't-make-it-another-minute days he all too often experienced. He knew the best antidote for it was sleep, and he was tempted to administer a very large dose of it to himself. *Plenty of time to sleep when all this is over with*, he thought. Until then, he knew he could recline the driver's side seat all the way back and at the very least close his eyes for a brief nap. After all, it wouldn't be the first time he'd spent the night catnapping in front of someone's house while conducting surveillance.

He was about to reach for the lever on the side of his seat and do just that when a black Lincoln Town Car turned off St. Charles and braked to a halt in the driveway of the rectory. A moment later Jack observed Father Edward Brennan stepping out on the passenger side of the vehicle. The priest turned back toward the car, leaned down, said something through the open door to the driver, and then closed it. He watched Father Brennan walk to the front door of the rectory, extract a key from his pocket, and unlock the door. Jack glanced down at his watch and saw it was twelve fifteen. *Getting home kind of late tonight, aren't you, Father?*

Jack was disappointed when he saw that no uniformed officers had accompanied the priest. It really didn't surprise him—he figured Sergeant Gillette at the New Orleans Police Department decided it wasn't important enough to send two of his officers to look after a priest when they could be more useful somewhere else. A minute or two later he saw one of the upper floor lights go on and he figured Father Brennan had made his way upstairs to his bedroom. Another fifteen minutes passed by and the light was turned off. *Looks like everybody has turned in for the night*, he thought. *About time I did, too. Everything's just going to have to wait a little while longer, I suppose.*

He turned over the ignition and the Camaro's engine came to life again. As he pulled onto St. Charles and turned toward the Pontchartrain Hotel and the bed that beckoned him, he looked toward the darkened rectory and said, "Sleep tight, Padre."

***

Jack drove past the Pontchartrain a few minutes after one in the morning, turned off St. Charles, and found one of the hotel's reserved parking lots on Carondelet. He slid the .45 back in the leather holster under his jacket, got out, and walked to the back of the Camaro and popped the trunk. He covered the shotgun and the .38, closed the trunk, then walked back to the door of the car and reached in and grabbed his duffel bag. He placed the Bible and shaving kit inside it and walked the block and a half to the hotel.

He entered the lobby and noticed the night clerk was manning the desk. The clerk looked up from whatever he was doing at the desk and smiled, but Jack avoided eye contact altogether with him. He really didn't want to talk to *anyone* at this ungodly hour, so he ignored the young man and walked over to the elevator and punched the button on the wall. He took the elevator to the fourth floor, got out, and followed the signs directing him toward his room. He unlocked the door, flipped on the light, looked around the room, and smiled. *Not quite the Monteleone*, he thought, *but it's pretty darn close.*

After a quick shower, he walked over to the small bar in the room and looked at the selection in front of him. He chose a mini bottle of Jack Daniel's, found a can of coke and some ice in the small fridge underneath the bar, and mixed himself a drink. He picked up the Friday edition of the *Times-Picayune* from the desk in the corner of the room, pulled the covers back on the bed, and leaned back against a couple of the pillows and opened the paper. He turned to the sports section and scanned the first page as he sipped his drink. There was nothing about the Saints, but there was plenty of coverage of the major league baseball teams around the nation. He didn't follow baseball, and finding nothing else of interest in the rest of the sports section or any of the other sections, he folded the paper, tossed it on the bed beside him, and got up. He walked over to the bar again and made a second Jack and Coke. He laid back down, flipped on the television, and quickly scanned through the channels while nursing the drink in his hand. Finding nothing of interest on the television set, either, he turned it off, downed the rest of the drink, and stretched out on the bed. Within minutes he was sound asleep.

He awoke at seven thirty, rubbed the sleep from his eyes, and walked over to the small bar and flipped the switch on the coffee maker that sat next to the tray of whiskey bottles. After a quick visit to the bathroom he laid back in the bed, thought about turning on the television, but decided to leave it off instead. He was quite surprised at the decent night's sleep he got—even if it was only five hours or so—and his mind was already racing. He wasn't ready yet to get dressed and go downstairs to the hotel's café for their pecan waffles and freshly squeezed orange juice; he'd hoped reading would help fill the time until he did. It might be a little while before someone on the staff would deliver the Saturday morning's edition of the paper to his door, however. Until then what else was there to read? He looked around the room and spotted the duffel bag and the Bible protruding from it and recalled the letter Father Brennan had tucked into the book. *Okay, Padre,* he thought. *Let's see what you have in there for me. I'll give it a shot. I guess I can at least look it over until the paper arrives.*

He got up, pulled out the Gideon's Bible, went back to the bed, and leaned back against the pillows. He found a piece of paper marked "1" protruding from the pages of the book and flipped it open to the third chapter of Romans. A brief handwritten note from Father Brennan directed him to read verses 23 through 26. He scanned down the page, found them, and read, "'For all have sinned and fall short of the glory of God, and are justified freely by his grace, through the redemption that came by Christ Jesus. God presented him as a sacrifice of atonement, through faith in his blood . . .'"

Old news, Father, he thought. *I'm quite familiar with all that. Remember, I grew up in the Church.*

He got up, poured a cup of coffee, stirred in some cream and sugar, and walked back to the bed. *Show me something new,* he thought as he laid back in the bed and picked up the Bible again. He read on. "'He did this to demonstrate his justice, because in his forbearance he had left the sins committed beforehand unpunished—he did it to demonstrate his justice at the present time, so as to be just and the one who justifies those who have faith in Jesus. . .'"

Don't recall that, he thought. *I like how it discusses the issue of justice.*

He found the paper marked "2" protruding from the pages of the book. Keeping Jack in Romans, Father Brennan's note directed him to verses 12 and 13 of chapter five. Jack read, "'Therefore, just as sin entered the world through one man, and death through sin, and in this way death came to all men, because all sinned—. For before the law was given, sin was in the world.'"

Jack read the note from Father Brennan written at the bottom of the piece of paper.

Jack,

I'm going to jump you around a bit now, but bear with me. There is a method to my madness. Read Romans 6:23, then go back to chapter 5, to verses 6–8. The apostle Paul laid it all out for us in Romans; all we have to do is pay attention to what God is telling us through this man.

With his interest piqued, Jack did as he was instructed. He flipped the pages and read, "For the wages of sin is death, but the gift of God is eternal life in Christ Jesus our Lord."

I know that one, too, he thought. *Learned it, along with all the other kids at St. Michael's. Father De Marco drilled it into our heads time and time again!*

Then he read on. "'You see, at just the right time, when we were still powerless, Christ died for the ungodly. Very rarely will anyone die for a righteous man, though for a good man someone might possibly dare to die. But God demonstrates his own love for us in this: While we were still sinners, Christ died for us.'"

Jack closed the book and held it in his left hand, sandwiching his index finger between the pages to hold the place where he left off. He stared at the back cover of the book, subconsciously rubbing it with his thumb. *So much there to chew on,* he thought, *especially all that about dying not for the righteous man but for a good man.* He flipped the book open again, and found Father Brennan's note on the bottom of the piece of paper marked "5," directing him next to Romans 10:9–13. He read them, then found number "6" for Romans 6:4, then 8–12. As he read those passages he thought that although they, too, sounded familiar, he felt he was actually reading them for the very first time.

He saw Father Brennan's note directing him to Romans 12:2 and also 21 and wondered what could be next. He found the chapter, and read Father Brennan's additional note tucked between the pages.

Jack,

This is where it begins to come together. Pay attention to what the Holy Spirit, through the writing of Paul, is urging you to do. It's so simple, yet we make it so complicated. After you've read it, there's something else I want you to read that Paul wrote. You'll find it in his second letter to the church at Corinth—it's Second Corinthians 5:17. It is my wish, my prayer, for you, Jack.

Take care, my friend!
Father Edward Brennan

Jack read, "'Do not conform any longer to the pattern of this world, but be transformed by the renewing of your mind. Then you will be able to test and approve what God's will is—his good, pleasing and perfect will. . .Do not be overcome by evil, but overcome evil with good.'" He flipped several pages forward until he found the second book of Corinthians. He immediately went to chapter 5 and scanned down the page until he found verse 17.

"'Therefore, if anyone is in Christ, he is a new creation; the old has gone, the new has come!'"Jack closed the Bible and placed it on the bed next to him. There were so many passages pointed out to him by the priest and he couldn't remember if he had read them or not as a boy. He picked up the Bible again, flipped it open, and began reading them once more. That led him to read many others, as well, and as he did so he lost track of time altogether.

***

He was lost in the passages, thinking deeply about them as he read, when something urged him to look over at the digital clock on the night-stand: *10:30*. He looked at it again, thinking perhaps his eyes were playing a trick on him: *10:30*. *Oh, my God!* he thought. He dropped the Bible on the bed and quickly headed for the bathroom. He needed to shave and get dressed, pack up and check out as quickly as he could. He chided himself for not paying attention to the time, for letting it slip by him as it did.

As he was shaving he formulated a quick plan. He figured it would be forty-five minutes, maybe even an hour, before he'd be at the church. He knew he'd have to skip the waffles at the café downstairs. Instead he would just get a couple of their blueberry muffins and a cup of juice and take it with him. He'd have to hustle over to his car and make his way through any Saturday morning traffic on St. Charles in order to get to the church as soon as he could. He was hoping against hope that Sal and Gino's men would take their time; maybe he'd get lucky and they'd eat a late breakfast wherever they were and get to the rectory and the church well after he arrived. He needed to beat them there, as the plan he was now running through his mind required time—to walk up to the front of the rectory and ring the doorbell until someone opened the door, then tell whoever answered he needed to speak with Father Brennan *immediately*. What he had to discuss with the priest just couldn't wait. He had far too many questions to ask him and he needed some answers right away.

CHAPTER 17

J ack arrived at the seven-thousand block of St. Charles Avenue at eleven thirty and drove slowly in front of the rectory next to the church. He immediately spotted a dark-grey Mercury Grand Marquis parked less than a block away from the church. There were two men in black suits sitting in the front seats, and Jack didn't figure them to be undercover cops. They appeared to be just the opposite, the kind he was most familiar with in his line of work. Professionals, plying their trade. *No need to have split up after all*, he thought. *It's Saturday, The Catholic Charities Office is closed. You're right where you should be, fellas. And so am I.*

Jack settled back in his seat, watching and waiting for the inevitable. Sooner or later they would make their move. He reached into the bag sitting on the seat next to him and pulled out the Bible and held it a moment in his hands. He had time to think. Time for other things, as well.

For the first time in years he began to pray.

***

An hour and a half passed and the two men had not moved from their seats in the Grand Marquis. It would be midafternoon before long, and he thought it was unusual for there to be so little activity at the rectory and at the church entrance, as well. He knew things should be picking up soon—confession was scheduled to begin at three-thirty, the Mass at five. He had seen only one New Orleans Police patrol car so far this afternoon. Apparently on routine patrol, it rolled right past the rectory and the church without even slowing down.

He had been counting on the New Orleans PD to be here; that was a big part of his plan. He recounted his conversation with Sergeant Gillette on the phone yesterday, how he had been very clear and very specific in telling him of his involvement in the abduction of Father Brennan and how he had hidden him, and that his life was in grave danger. He knew there'd be the chance they wouldn't take him seriously, but when he told Gillette exactly who and what he was and when he gave him his client's name, he figured they would have little choice but to protect the priest. The Russo brothers were well known throughout New Orleans for their mob connections and it should be no surprise to the NOPD they were involved in something of this nature. The question was, would they take him at his word that he was hired to kill Father Brennan? When he hung up the phone at the welcome center he had the sinking feeling he was being labeled as just another raving lunatic. *This is not good*, Jack thought as he sat in his car. *I need the police to be here.*

***

Another hour passed. He saw that the two gunmen were still sitting in their car. He glanced at the front of the rectory again and saw the front door swing open. He saw Father Brennan step through the open doorway, then stop and turn as if he was going to go back inside. But he only stood in the doorway, and it appeared to Jack the priest was speaking. Was he saying something to someone inside? It was too far away for him to be certain.

Jack turned back to watch the men in the Grand Marquis, and saw they had exited the vehicle and were walking across the road to the church entrance. He saw them pull their guns out from under their jackets; he quickly got out of the Camaro, pulled out his .45, and darted across the street to confront them.

"Father, get back inside!" Jack yelled in the direction of the priest as he ran onto the sidewalk.

"Jack?" Father Brennan yelled back. "What—what are you doing?" he asked as he began walking forward. A stocky, heavyset New Orleans Police officer emerged from the doorway, saw the two men charging toward the priest with weapons drawn, and ran forward and pulled him to the ground. A second uniformed officer, taller and thinner than the first, quickly emerged from the rectory, drew his service revolver, and darted toward Jack and the other two men. The first officer arose and left Father Brennan lying on the ground as he ran forward to assist his partner. Suddenly, both officers stopped, crouched, and aimed their Smith & Wesson .38s at Jack and the two gunmen. "Freeze!" they yelled.

Jack ignored their commands and instead kept his eyes fixed on the two men in front of him. He continued to run toward them and saw each of them level their handguns at him. He aimed for the gun hand of the one to his right and fired; the impact of the bullet shattered the man's right hand and he immediately dropped his weapon. The second hit man, seeing what had just happened, aimed at the upper torso of Jack and got off two quick rounds. The bullets from his .357 Magnum slammed into Jack's chest; he staggered forward and fell hard to the ground. The wounded gunman bent down, picked up his gun with his left hand, and aimed it at the shorter of the two officers. The second gunman also took aim, pointing his gun at the taller officer. As he lay face down on the ground, clutching his chest, Jack heard both officers yell for the shooters to drop their weapons, but he knew those commands would be ignored.

Several shots rang out as the men in front of him fired their weapons and the police officers behind him fired theirs, as well. Jack raised his head to watch the two gunmen get hit and fall forward to the sidewalk. He heard his name called out from somewhere behind him. He recognized the voice of Father Brennan. *Thank you, God. He's all right*, he thought as he closed his eyes.

***

Father Brennan arose from the ground and began running toward the men lying on the ground in front of him. As he drew closer the heavyset cop reached out and grabbed him, stopping him. The tall cop cautiously approached the three men lying on the ground in front of him. He kicked aside the weapons of the two gunmen and leaned down and checked each of them for a pulse.

"This one's gone," he called out. Then, "So's this one."

The heavyset cop then said, "Wait here, Father, while I search the other one." He knelt beside Jack and rolled him over onto his back and heard his labored breath. He did a quick search of him, then scanned the ground around him until he located the .45. "This one's alive. Just barely," he said to his partner. Then with a puzzled look on his face, he added, "He only fired to wound the first guy. Why didn't he just waste him instead?"

"I don't get it, either," the taller cop said. "It's almost like he was wanting us to do it for him."

Father Brennan moved forward and knelt beside Jack. Blood was running out of the corners of Jack's mouth, forming thin, crimson lines as it trickled down his cheeks. Father Brennan reached into his coat pocket and drew out a white handkerchief. He cupped the back of Jack's head with his right hand and lifted his head slightly; with his left hand, he gently wiped the blood from Jack's mouth with the handkerchief. "Jack, what were you thinking, running at those men like that?" he said. "That was a foolish thing for a man like you to do."

Jack coughed as he spoke. "I couldn't let them kill you, Father. . .and I. . . I'm just glad those cops were here." His breath was labored, and his blood soon saturated the white handkerchief. "After what we talked about yesterday, and. . ." he coughed again. ". . .after what I read in that Bible I. . . I couldn't do it anymore." He drew in a breath, then added, "That part, about. . .dying for a good man. . .I don't mind at all. . .for you." His coughing was hard now, and he drew a deeper, more ragged breath. More blood flowed down his cheeks. He gripped the priest's arm tighter, and looked directly into his eyes as he said, "I asked God to forgive me today, Father. I wanted to talk to you about it. . .but. . .it didn't work out. . .the way I planned."

"I'm sorry I wasn't there for you, Jack. But I'm here now. For as long as you need me."

"That's good. Do you think. . .God can. . .forgive someone like me, Father?"

"If you are *truly* sorry for your sins then, yes, Jack, He can. And He will."

Jack gripped Father Brennan's left arm even tighter with his hands. "I *am* sorry, Father. I'm *so very* sorry for what I've done," he replied. After another ragged cough, and more blood oozed out of the corners of his mouth, Jack asked, "Will you hear my last confession, Father?"

Before the priest had a chance to answer, Jack coughed once more. He drew in a final breath, then released it slowly. Father Brennan felt the pressure on his arm lighten; he noticed that Jack's eyes stared vacantly into the cloudless blue sky overhead.

"There's no need to, my friend," Father Brennan said aloud. "God has heard it. He has forgiven you of your sins."

The two policemen who had been standing nearby watched as the priest knelt over the dying man who was lying on the ground in front of them. They knew the man was bleeding out and there was nothing that could be done to save him. They watched the priest comfort him, and after the man had taken his last breath they watched the priest gently lower his head to the ground. They saw him reach his hand inside his coat and remove a long, thin piece of purple cloth; the priest pressed it to his lips and then draped it around his neck. The taller of the two policemen watched as the priest made a motion with his right hand in the form of a cross over the man lying on the ground. He leaned in and listened intently to the priest as he spoke.

"In the name of the Father, the Son, and the Holy Spirit," he heard him say.

The taller policeman leaned in toward his shorter partner. "Al, you're Catholic, aren't you?" he whispered. "What's he doing?"

"He's administering the Last Rites of the Church, Jerry," Al replied.

"Oh," Jerry replied. After a brief pause he asked, "Why's it done?"

"I'll explain it later. Just be quiet for now. Show some respect," he told his partner.

They continued to watch as the priest placed his left hand on Jack's chest and held his right hand up. They stood motionless as they heard the priest speak again.

"May the Lord in His love and mercy help you with the Grace of the Holy Spirit, and may the Lord who frees you from your sins save you and raise you up. Amen."

The two policemen stood motionless, waiting for the priest to speak again. A minute passed in awkward silence; when another went by it was obvious nothing more was forthcoming from him.

"I'll go call this one in," Jerry stated.

"Yeah. You better go ahead and do that," Al replied. "Three dead. There's gonna be an awful lot of paperwork on this one." When Jerry turned in the direction of the rectory and the patrol car that was parked beyond it, Al added, "Tell Dispatch there's no need to rush on the ambulances. No doctor's gonna help them where they're goin'."

A gentle breeze blew in and stirred the heavy, humid air. Somewhere in the distance a dog barked, and a mockingbird sang from a nearby Dogwood tree. Al leaned over and placed a hand on the priest's right shoulder.

"Father, why don't you go with Officer Mitchell?" he said. "He'll see to it that you get inside the rectory there before he goes to the squad car and calls this in. "I have to stay here until my shift sergeant gets here with the investigating team. Nothing more any of us can do for them."

Father Brennan clutched the blood-soaked handkerchief in his hand as he walked toward the rectory. He stopped, turned toward Al, and asked, "What time is it, Officer?"

Al looked at his watch. "It's a little after two, Father," he replied.

"That's good," Father Brennan said. "I still have time to get ready for this afternoon's confession and Mass." Then he continued walking toward the rectory.

Al called after the priest. "You did all you could, Father. He's in God's hands now."

"Yes, he is. He *is* in God's hands," Father Brennan said to himself as he continued to walk toward the rectory.

EPILOGUE

New Orleans
April 2011

Father Thomas Poncelet, the newly appointed pastor of St. Patrick's Catholic Church on Camp Avenue, concluded the second reading of the Mass from the Epistle of Paul to the Galatians, leaned forward, and lightly kissed one of the open pages of the Bible that lay on the podium in front of him. He turned and stepped off the raised dais. He stopped, bowed toward His Excellency the Most Reverend Edward J. Brennan, and walked toward the altar to join him there. He took his seat to the right of Bishop Brennan, who nodded and smiled at him as he did so. Bishop Brennan then turned to his left, nodded, and smiled at Father James O'Connor, the long-time pastor of the Church of the Sacred Heart of Jesus. After the Gospel Acclamation was completed by the audience, Father O'Connor rose from his seat, walked down the steps of the altar, and stepped up onto the dais.

Bishop Brennan was thinking how wonderful it was that his two closest friends were here to concelebrate his retirement Mass, and was grateful that the archbishop had granted him special permission for it to be held here at the Church of the Sacred Heart, his former parish, instead of requiring him to say it at the St. Louis Cathedral in the Quarter. He scanned the crowded church and recognized many of his former parishioners were in attendance, along with a number of officials and dignitaries from the archdiocese. He then looked to his right and watched as Father O'Connor turned the pages of the Bible to begin his reading of the Gospel. Father O'Connor led the congregation in the sign of the cross and then spoke.

"The Lord be with you," he said.

"And also with you," the audience responded.

"A reading from the Holy Gospel according to Luke," Father O'Connor stated. "Jesus said, 'There was a man who had two sons. And the younger of them said to his father, Father give me the share of the property that is coming to me. And he divided his property between them. Not many days later the younger son gathered all he had and took a journey into a far country. And there he squandered his property in reckless living. . .'"

As Father O'Connor continued reading from the Gospel of Luke, Bishop Brennan again scanned the faces of those in the congregation, and tears began to form in the corners of his eyes. This was a day long in coming—he had reached the mandated retirement age of seventy-five and was now here to officiate at his last Mass; now that it was upon him he wished he had more time. *I'm too young to be forced into retirement,* he thought. *I don't want to be like one of those cowboys who just goes and rides off into the sunset, never to be seen again. There are other ways I can still serve the Lord.*

He looked over at Father O'Connor and smiled as he listened to his friend concluding his reading of the Parable of the Lost Son.

"'. . .It was fitting to celebrate and be glad, for this your brother was dead, and is alive; he was lost, and is found.' This is the Gospel of the Lord."

"Praise to you, Lord Jesus Christ," the audience replied as Father O'Connor stepped down from the dais and returned to his seat at the altar.

His Excellency the Most Reverend Edward Brennan then arose from the center chair, turned to his right, walked down the steps of the altar, and then up the short steps of the dais that faced the congregation. He steeled himself, fought back more tears, and spoke.

"Thank you for coming here this beautiful spring day," the retiring auxiliary bishop of New Orleans and vicar-general said. "Before I begin my homily on what you have just heard—the Parable of the Lost Son—I would like to say to so many of you in attendance that it has been my privilege to have served you as your associate pastor, then your pastor, not so long ago at this very church. I recognize so many of you today, and I see you have retained your youthful vigor, as have I."

There was a ripple of laughter throughout the audience and he waited a moment before he spoke again.

"But there comes a time in every man's life when, to borrow a well-worn phrase, he has to 'hang up his spurs,' and so it is that I come before you to do just that. It is with both sadness and joy that I leave all of you now, having so faithfully served our Lord Jesus Christ and you in my present capacity under the direction of our beloved archbishop. Please be assured that, even though I must step down from my role as auxiliary bishop and vicar-general for the archdiocese, I will continue to serve our Heavenly Father and you during my retirement years."

He scanned the crowd and gathered himself. He knew he had to be steady and calm, that he would have to work hard just to keep his emotions in check for what he had to say in his message to them.

"Now, if you will, please allow me to give you my humble interpretation of this wonderful parable as told by our Blessed Savior; in so doing, please allow me also to take you back in time with me, to an April day thirty years ago. In so doing I will tell you of an encounter I had with one of those lost sons, a man by the name of Jack Brantley. If you will be patient with me, I will tell you the story not only of how this prodigal son saved my life, but more importantly, I will tell you how Our Heavenly Father saved his."

ACKNOWLEDGMENTS

There are a number of people I want to express my sincere appreciation to in the writing of this novel. I especially want to thank my wife, Lee Anne, and my daughters, Caroline and Emilee, for their advice, encouragement, prayers and reading of the initial and final drafts of the manuscript. A special thanks goes out to Katherine Wiggins, a young lady Lee Anne and I had the privilege of teaching for a number of years in Sunday School at McDonough Road Baptist Church in Fayetteville, Georgia; Katherine, I always looked forward to hearing you ask, "How's the book coming along?" Other thanks go out to members of McDonough Christian Church in McDonough, Georgia: Andy Daugherty, for your advice on the publishing process; Michael White, for your enthusiasm and prayers for the publication of this novel; and to the guys in my "Joshua's Men" group, David Langford, Eddie Starrett, Jim Rast, and Robert Williams—many thanks for your prayers for me each time we met. Most of all, a special thanks goes to Royce and Ann Aultman for their friendship to my wife and me, for their continual encouragement and prayers, and for their support in getting this book published.

CPSIA information can be obtained
at www.ICGtesting.com
Printed in the USA
LVHW081134270319
612009LV00004B/8/P